TANGO

Steel Patriots MC

Book SIX

Mary Kennedy

III

INSATIABLE INK

CHAPTER ONE

Tyler "Tango" Green shifted uncomfortably from one foot to the other. His uniform was suffocating him in this heat, the collar itching his neck, the sweat dripping slowly down his back. At six-foot-two and two hundred and thirty-five pounds, he wasn't the tallest or the heaviest man on his team, but he was probably the most solidly packed with muscle. Tango loved the gym and loved staying in shape. Partly it was a desire to have pride in his body, but it was also a necessity to ensure he was capable of helping his teammates if needed.

None of that really mattered at this moment. At this moment, he wasn't being judged on how good he looked or how strong he was; he wasn't being judged on his fifteen-year career that contained some of the toughest missions known to the military. No, today, he stood before a review panel who didn't know shit from shinola, and yet they were judging the team on actions taken during a mission.

Tango stood before the military action and disciplinary review board, waiting as the four men perused the paperwork before them, asked one another questions but had yet to ask him anything. His thoughts traveled to his little apartment back home where his baby, his motorcycle, lay waiting for him; her gleaming tank painted by him; the

engine put together by his hands. He couldn't wait to put her between his

legs once again and ride that girl up and down the East Coast.

Instead, he was standing here before men that hadn't done the

job he was performing in decades, if ever. He was being judged by men

who had no comprehension of what it was like to see twelve innocent,

tiny little bodies hanging from a cliff. Bodies who had been shown no

mercy, no justice, bodies that would haunt his thoughts for a lifetime.

He was a United States Navy SEAL. The most elite warriors

known to man, and he was proud to serve on a team of like-minded elite

warriors from all branches of service. The team led by Eric "Ghost"

Stanton, also a SEAL, was made up of SEALs, Army Rangers, and MARSOC.

All the best trained, the most feared warriors of their class. Each man

hand-selected by Ghost to serve on a team where they would be called to

perform missions others could not do or refused to do. Their record was

stellar, their success rate one hundred percent. Until this mission.

This mission, they'd received spotty intelligence and

communication from an Army intelligence officer who was not their

normal conduit for intel. This guy looked as though he'd barely finished boot camp, and the way he hung his head at the table indicated to Tango that he knew he was partly at fault for the poor information.

He tried to wait patiently for the men to speak, killing the time by reciting his credo:

In times of war or uncertainty there is a special breed of warrior ready to answer our Nation's call. A common man with uncommon desire to succeed.

Forged by adversity, he stands alongside America's finest special operations forces to serve his country, the American people, and protect their way of life.

I am that man.

My Trident is a symbol of honor and heritage. Bestowed upon me by the heroes that have gone before, it embodies the trust of those I have sworn to protect. By wearing the Trident, I accept the responsibility of my chosen profession and way of life. It is a privilege that I must earn every day.

My loyalty to Country and Team is beyond reproach. I humbly serve as a guardian to my fellow Americans always ready to defend those who are unable to defend themselves. I do not advertise the nature of my work, nor seek recognition for my actions. I voluntarily accept the inherent hazards of my profession, placing the welfare and security of others before my own.

I serve with honor on and off the battlefield. The ability to control my emotions and my actions, regardless of circumstance, sets me apart from other men.

Uncompromising integrity is my standard. My character and honor are steadfast. My word is my bond.

We expect to lead and be led. In the absence of orders, I will take charge, lead my teammates and accomplish the mission. I lead by example in all situations.

I will never quit. I persevere and thrive on adversity. My Nation expects me to be physically harder and mentally stronger than my enemies. If knocked down, I will get back up, every time. I will draw on every remaining ounce of strength to protect my teammates and to accomplish our mission. I am never out of the fight.

We demand discipline. We expect innovation. The lives of my teammates and the success of our mission depend on me – my technical *skill, tactical proficiency, and attention to detail. My training is never*

complete.

We train for war and fight to win. I stand ready to bring the full

spectrum of combat power to bear in order to achieve my mission and the

goals established by my country. The execution of my duties will be swift

and violent when required yet guided by the very principles that I serve to

defend.

Brave men have fought and died building the proud tradition and

feared reputation that I am bound to uphold. In the worst of conditions,

the legacy of my teammates steadies my resolve and silently guides my

every deed.

I will not fail.

"You will not fail at what?" asked Admiral Crossing. "Petty

officer? You said you will not fail. What did you mean?"

Tango hadn't realized he said the last sentence aloud, but he

knew in his gut it was a sign that he needed to express this thought aloud

to the panel.

"I simply was stating part of my credo, Admiral Crossing. I will not

fail. Every SEAL knows those words. This was our mission, and although the intel fed to us was less than ideal, we performed our mission with honor and integrity. I did not fail. I, my team and I brought justice for those children and their families."

"Petty Officer is it your belief that you had no other viable alternative in this mission?" asked General Whitman.

"I believe that with every fiber of my being, sir. We performed our mission as directed. We returned those poor children to their parents and brought justice to the killers. If we had received the information in a timelier manner, had we known that this was not a ransom issue but a rescue mission, our tactics and the outcome might have been very different. But we'll never know that, will we, sirs?" Tango stared directly at the Army intelligence officer, who squirmed under his gaze.

"Do you have any regrets, Petty Officer Green?" said Admiral Crossing.

"None, other than we didn't find those children alive," said Tango.

"Thank you, Petty Officer Green," said Crossing. "You can step outside and wait with your teammates while we finish with the others."

Tango stepped into the hallway pulling at his collar, sweat rolling down the back of his neck. He looked at his teammates and murmured 'fucking witch hunt' as he took his seat. He waited as each man told his story, and then Jack "Doc" Harris was called.

Because of the shitty construction of the building, they could hear everything being said inside the room, and when Jack "Doc" Harris notified the members of the panel that he possessed photos of the girls. They all stirred a bit in their seats. Taking photos of prisoners, dead bodies, anything to do with a mission was strictly forbidden unless directed to do so. Doc could be placing a noose on all their necks, or he could be saving them.

Doc stepped outside the room and stared at his teammates, nodding at them to walk with him to the end of the hallway.

"Fucking hell, Doc, we didn't know you had photos," said Ghost.

"I know. I took them when we were cutting the girls down. Don't ask me why. I know it's a violation, but I just had this feeling and shit for luck, it paid off."

"Well," said Razor, "I, for one, am fucking eternally grateful. They won't court-martial us with the fear of those photos becoming public. The liberals would be screaming about human rights, and the conservatives would say the killing of those men was justified. They don't want to have to argue that."

"This shit is getting fucking exhausting," said Ghost. "I'm so damned tired of having to follow rules created by men who don't do the damn job anymore, or for that matter, ever did the job." They all nodded as the doors of the hearing room opened once again. The MP waved them inside.

Standing before the committee, the men all removed their hats and stood at attention.

"Gentlemen, you have presented us with a dilemma, and I won't lie. It's one I hate," said Admiral Crossing. "Your work as a unit has been indisputable, but we are getting pressures from the country's government claiming you murdered innocent men."

Tango wanted desperately to remove his jacket. He was literally suffocating under the weight of the material and the rows of ribbons and medals. Maybe it was a metaphor for what he was truly feeling.

"I didn't say I agree. However, we are tasked with making a show of, hell, I don't even know anymore. We are asking you to retire, gentlemen. If you refuse, you will be dishonorably discharged. If you take the retirement, there will be no mark on your records. It saddens me to do this, to lose some of the finest men I know and that I know we need in our service."

"I accept retirement," said Tango quickly.

The chorus was heard down the line as each man agreed, regrettably. The Admiral nodded at them, handing them their papers that would tell administration they were taking retirement effective immediately.

"You will be expected to be packed and on the next transport home within forty-eight hours. I wish you good luck, men. The world needs people like you. I hope you find a way to continue to the good fight."

Thirty-three hours later, they were seated in the back of a transport on their way home. Their bags packed, their papers in hand, and no clue what they would do next. Seven of the most elite, deadliest warriors ever to serve out of a job.

"Where will you go, Ghost?" asked Whiskey. Ghost looked at the men he'd called teammates for the last decade. Each man was hand-selected for his team, partly because he knew of their skills but mostly because he trusted them with his life and the lives of every member of the team.

"I have a proposition for all of you. I know some of you have family back home, but nobody has an old lady that I'm aware of," he said, smirking at the men on the transport.

"Well, Tango has a mule he's fond of," said Doc with a smile.

"Fuck you, Doc, at least it's a female mule," he grinned. "So, what's your point, Ghost?"

"My point is, when my pops died, he left me a huge piece of land. It's nothing special, but it's got an old garage on the property where he used to repair cars, bikes, tractors, shit like that for neighbors. The house burned down years ago, but Pops made the barn into a pretty livable space."

"SOOO, you want us all to live there?" asked Gunner.

"Like share bunk beds or some shit?" questioned Zulu.

"No, I mean, yea. Look, I ride, you all know that, and I know that most of you do too. What if we formed our own club... motorcycle club? We pick a name, make the garage something that we can all work, and maybe open a bar or some shit."

The men all looked at one another, nodding. It was a good idea, but not one of them knew anything about running a business or a bar.

"I'm in," said Tango, "but I know jack-shit about operating a bar. I can fix anything with a motor, and so can most of you, but a bar? I don't know, man. I know *how* to drink, just not how to mix drinks."

"Look, it doesn't have to happen right away. MCs are pretty territorial. We need to make sure we're not stepping on anyone's toes. I'm not a fan of becoming an outlaw MC. We got our taste of outlaw in that fucking shithole we just came from, and it didn't do any of us any good. I'm suggesting that between the bar and the garage, we'll have two legitimate businesses. Maybe on the side, we sort of informally help people."

"Help people? Like good Samaritans?" asked Gunner.

"Sort of, I'm thinking more like we take jobs others won't, but only the ones we want to take. We find lost kids, kidnap victims, we help the old lady being screwed over by a nasty landlord, shit like that." The men all looked at him, raising their eyebrows. "Look, I know we've spent our entire careers doing just this kind of shit, but now we get to do it on our terms. The shop needs cleaning up, and the barn will need to be made inhabitable – adding more electrical, plumbing – but it's huge. I've got a shit ton of money saved from all my deployments, and Pops left me a nice little chunk of change."

"And we'd be partners?" asked Whiskey.

"Yea, we'd be fucking partners. We'd be brothers, asshole," he said with a grin. "Just like we are now. We'd rely on one another and do shit our way. No red tape, no governments telling us what to do. We ride our fucking bikes when we want; we take the jobs we want; we fuck who we want, and we drink 'til we can't drink no more." The men smiled in his direction.

"I'm in," said Tango.

"Me too," said Doc.

"Why the fuck not?" said Razor.

"Fuck, you know I'm in, asshole," said Gunner.

"I guess we need a name," said Whiskey. "How about Steel Soldiers?"

"No fucking way, asshole. I'm a SEAL, not a fucking soldier," said Tango. The others laughed and nodded. They were all from different branches of the military and loved teasing each other about the superiority of their own branch, but deep down held mad respect for one another.

"Steel Patriots," said Ghost. "The steel between our legs, and the fucking patriot spirit we all still carry."

"Steel Patriots," whispered Whiskey. The others nodded and smiled.

"Steel Patriots it is."

CHAPTER TWO

Twenty years earlier...

Taylor grabbed her cereal bowl and moved around the sofa to sit and watch the morning news. She wasn't really a news junkie at fourteen years old, but it was part of a homework assignment for school. Her stepbrother's long legs were sprawled across the coffee table, blocking her path.

"Can you please move your legs, Evan?" she asked nicely. He looked up at her, leering, taking in her lithe, strong little body. The perfect student, perfect daughter, perfect cheerleader.

"Why don't you just sit on my legs?" he said with a disgusting smile.

"Don't be gross, Evan. I'm your sister," she said, shoving his legs. He reached up quickly, grabbing her thighs, and pulling her toward him, cereal spilling everywhere. "Evan!"

"You're my stepsister," he said, gripping her thighs tightly, "that means we can fuck, and no one will care."

"Stop it!" she said, pushing against him. "Stop it, Evan! I swear I'm gonna tell Mom!" He pressed his fingers into her soft flesh, and she could feel him harden beneath. Panic bubbled in her chest as he held her against his hardening dick.

"Go ahead. Yell, pretty girl. Your mom and my father are gone... all weekend. That's right, precious, they decided on a quick getaway this morning, leaving you in my charge," he said, running his tongue along the side of her neck.

Oh God! Oh shit! What the hell was she going to do now? She could run to a neighbor or friend's house, but he was holding her so tightly she wasn't sure she could get away. At only five-foot-two and barely a hundred pounds, Evan had a good eight inches and another seventy pounds of weight on her. He was eighteen to her fourteen, and since the day he and his father moved into their home, he'd been staring at her, walking into her room without knocking, watching her at cheerleading practice. He creeped the shit out of Taylor, but every time she brought it up with her mother, she claimed he was only being a protective older brother.

Taylor screamed, and he slapped her again, his body making horrible grunting sounds, writhing against her.

"That's it. You like that, don't you?" he said, kissing her face again. "You like it, and you know it. Yea, baby, I knew you'd be a tight little pussy, fucking take it, you little tease." Taylor couldn't look at him, couldn't stand to see his face as he grunted and groaned, finally collapsing on top of her. She felt a warm liquid oozing from her and began to cry.

Evan stood in front of her, his penis coated in a creamy, bloody substance. He looked down at it and grinned. Taylor tried to get off the sofa, but he shoved her back down.

"Not so fast, bitch. That was better than I thought it was gonna be," he said, twisting her long ponytail. "I think you and I should have our own getaway this weekend." Taylor started to sob, reaching for her clothes.

"Evan, no, let me go. I won't say anything. I p-promise... please let me go," she begged.

"I'll let you go when I'm done with you," he sneered, pulling her off the couch. He walked toward the garage and shoved her in the backseat of the car.

"Evan, let me get some clothes," she pleaded.

"You won't need any fucking clothes where we're going, bitch," he said as tires squealed out of the driveway. Taylor closed her eyes, sobbing in the backseat, her body already bruising and bleeding. Why? Why was he doing this to her? She'd tried to be a good stepsister; she'd tried to be nice to him. At school, he would ignore her or tease her, but as a senior and her a freshman, he pretty much ruled the school.

He didn't need to do this. He had plenty of girls falling all over him. Why do this to her? When the car finally stopped, Taylor looked up to see the battered cabin once belonging to Evan's grandfather. Their parents brought them out here a year ago, saying they were planning to fix it up for a summer getaway. Now Taylor knew it would be the place she died.

Three days later, she woke on the floor of the cabin. Her body was black and blue, not an inch of pink flesh showing. Her vagina was torn, ripped from repeated raping and abuse. Semen coated her body, mixed with blood, her hair dried and matted to her head. Silence filled the small space, and Taylor knew this would be the last thing she ever saw.

She thought of her grandparents and their small coffee shop and bakery, her happy place. She wouldn't get to tell them how much she loved them; she wouldn't be able to tell them how sorry she was. There would be no high school dances, no college, no husband, no babies. She was dying. She closed her eyes. In the distance, hearing screaming and the sounds of sirens.

When Taylor opened her eyes once again, she was lying in a hospital room, her mother on one side, her stepfather on the other. His face was difficult to read, seemingly filled with pain and disappointment, her mother's similar. Two police officers were at the foot of her bed.

"Taylor," whispered her mother. "Oh, honey, we're so sorry we left you with him, so very sorry." Taylor just turned her head away from her mother, closing her eyes. They'd known that Evan was watching her, being mean, and yet they didn't do anything.

"Is he... is h-he gone?" asked Taylor. The officer at the foot of her bed nodded.

"He's been arrested and will face charges as an adult, Taylor. We'll need to get a statement from you, but that can wait," she said with a small smile.

"No. N-no, I need to tell you now… everything." She looked at her parents and shook her head. "Alone. I want to do it without them." The officer nodded, her parents not even protesting. Two hours later, with the statements given, the rape kits complete, a myriad of tests and procedures done to ensure that Taylor would be disease free as well negate any possibility of pregnancy, she was lying in the hospital bed alone.

The thought of returning to her parents' home brought painful sobs from her tiny body. Picking up the phone in her room, she dialed the number of the only people in the world she trusted.

"G-grandma…"

"Oh, my sweet baby girl, do you need me to come and get you?" she asked.

"Y-yes, can I live with you?" she asked. She heard her grandmother talking to her grandfather, her voice calm and reassuring.

"We'll find a way."

CHAPTER THREE

Present Day...

Taylor looked at the calendar and shuddered seeing the date. Fifty-two days. Fifty-two days before her stepbrother had the possibility of being released on parole. She'd pleaded her case to the parole board, begged for him to remain incarcerated, and yet still, she'd heard nothing about his pending release. Twenty years... twenty years of her life, she'd looked over her shoulder.

He'd taken everything from her in those three days. Everything. Her innocence, her virginity, her spirit, her parents. Although neither seemed to outwardly blame her for what happened to Evan, they both claimed that she should have been more careful about what she wore. If her dress was above the knees, they would give her a look. If her makeup was more than usual, she would get a sigh.

Her grandparents were the only people who kept her sane. Refusing to return to the home where he'd attacked her, she moved in with the elderly couple right away, living with them for almost a year before her parents finally sold the house and moved.

She tried living with them again, but it was almost worse. Whenever she could, she'd spend time with her grandparents working in the shop. When she left for college, she simply moved in with them and never returned to her parents' home. She'd closed herself off from other people, other than casual interactions in the coffee shop.

Six months ago, everything changed. A little after eight on a Saturday morning, a devastatingly handsome man walked into her shop. Clad in jeans, leather chaps, a tight t-shirt, and the most amazing smile, she nearly fell over. His hair was neatly trimmed, his goatee sexy beyond her imagination. She desperately wanted to reach out and stroke that face but didn't dare.

He ordered coffee and a muffin, ate it in silence, and then waved casually as he left. He returned three days later and ordered the same. It was another month before he asked her name, and she got his – Tango.

Taylor had a few dates in the last twenty years, but none managed to go beyond two or three dates. She just couldn't. She couldn't make herself tell them her terrible secret. But this man, this man who was so strikingly beautiful, made her head spin with desire and possibility.

Now he was in her shop asking her on a date.

"So, Taylor, I was wondering. We're having a big Fourth of July celebration out at the barn. Would you like to..."

"Yes!" she said excitedly and then blushed. Tango laughed and nodded at her. "Sorry. Yes. I've been hoping you'd ask me out."

"Wish you woulda told me, honey," he grinned. "I was thinking I'm too old for you."

"Too old? Tango, just how old do you think I am?" she asked. He perused her tiny little body, all that cute as shit curly, blonde hair a mess on her head; her tiny little waist leading to perfect little breasts.

"I don't know, mid-twenties?"

"You're sweet Tango, but I'm thirty-four." His eyes went wide, and he smiled even wider. "Can I ask your real name?"

"Tyler."

"Tyler," she repeated, extending her hand, "it's nice to meet you, Tyler. I'm Taylor, and I look forward to spending the Fourth with you." Tango was lost for words. He stood there just holding her hand when the guy behind him nudged him.

"Buddy, you gonna let go of her hand so I can get my damned coffee?" Tango turned, giving the man a look of death, and then turned back to Taylor, giving her a wink.

"I'll be back at lunch, to eat, I mean, and to see you," he said, walking out the door. Taylor graced him with a huge smile helping the man waiting for his coffee.

"A date," she whispered as she poured the man's coffee. "Oh God, I have a date."

CHAPTER FOUR

Tango couldn't believe he'd finally worked up the nerve to ask the little blonde out on a date. He'd been visiting that damned coffee shop for nearly six months now, ordering coffee and a muffin every time. The muffins were good, but he sure as shit wasn't a huge muffin guy. It was the company he wanted to be around.

He knew that Taylor took over the shop when her grandparents died. He knew that she had a strained relationship with her mom and stepdad, but that was pretty much all he knew.

Now with Gunner's woman owning the bookstore next door, and him being attached at the hip not only to her but that adorable little girl, it gave Tango all the more reason to be around Taylor.

Ideally, he should have his ass at the shop working on their custom bikes. That was his happy place, his hands in grease and gears. Razor was in charge of the custom paint, but the motors, those were his babies. Ironic, he thought, that Taylor made edible creations with her hands, and he made moving creations with his own.

When the shit went down at the bookstore, and he asked her to close up early, she'd trusted him. When she came back to work, and he promised all would be well, she'd trusted him. Now she was in the hands of an asshole who might very well blow her up, and she was looking at him like she trusted him again.

They'd waited for the man known as Javier Ascencio to pull up, hoping to end this shit they found in the attic of the bookstore. When pressed by Gunner, though, he revealed that he did indeed have the upper hand.

Lying in the back of the van was Calla and Taylor, both strapped with suicide vests, their mouths taped shut with duct tape. Tango's chest tightened at the sight of those blue eyes filled with fear and tears, yet there was something else too, a desire to survive.

"Uh, uh, uh," he said, smiling. "You take one step toward me; you even think about allowing those men to shoot at me; they will be dead before the bullet hits." Tango stared into the eyes of Taylor, tears streaking her face, but she tried to get closer to Calla, comforting the little girl. All this fucked up mess, and all she wanted to do was protect and comfort Calla.

"Take the tape off the girl. She's too little to know to breathe through her nose," said Gunner.

"Oh, you mean your soon-to-be daughter?" he said, grinning. "You see, I know everything, every... thing. I will take the tape off, but if she cries, I will place it back on." Gunner nodded as he pulled the tape roughly from her mouth. She gasped for air, her tears falling more freely down her face. Tango couldn't take his eyes off of Taylor, trying to tell her all would be okay, willing her to trust him.

"Daddy Uncle Tango," she cried.

"It's okay, baby. Daddy and Uncle Tango are going to get you," he said, trying to calm the little girl.

"That's right," said Javier, "Daddy and Uncle Tango are going to give Mr. Javier everything he's asked for, and then, maybe, they can have you back in little tiny pieces."

"You touch them," said Tango, staring at Taylor, her big blue eyes wet with tears, "you lay one finger, disturb one hair on their heads, and I'll fucking kill you."

"Such language in front of the child. You do realize that I could have them sold and on a ship before you two even know where I've taken them. You see, I have endless resources, endless, which is why Bashiir contacted me. The problem is that idiot at the shipping store went and died on me without telling me where everything was stashed. Then that pretty woman of yours buys the building, and I can't get in without creating an issue.

"So, here's what's going to happen. You're going to bring the drugs, the cases, and the dynamite to me by noon tomorrow, or they're both dead."

"The dynamite was blown the other night. It was unstable," said Gunner. Javier nodded.

"Fine, replace it with C4. We both know you have access to it. Bring an equal number of blocks of C4 along with the cases and the drugs." He started to round the van then turned to the two men. "If you try to follow me, if you even think about coming after me, well, it would be such a shame to let a buyer have these two beauties."

Gunner watched as the van drove away and collapsed to his knees. Tango rushed to his side. He was struggling to get enough air in his lungs, his hand shaking violently at his sides.

"Brother, we have to go. We have to find them," said Tango.

"No, we can't risk them. We can't risk either of them," he said as the other men came running toward them. "Fuck." He cried.

"We'll find them," said Ghost. "We'll find them."

"Hey, does anyone want to know where the van is heading?"

It was the voice of the ever-faithful Ace.

"You know where he's going?" said Gunner into his mouthpiece.

"Uh, yea, that's what you guys pay me for. I linked into his phone and GPS while he was chatting with you guys. He's about ten miles north, headed to the West Virginia border."

"Keep tracking him, Ace. We're going to follow at a distance, but let us know when he stops," said Ghost. "And, Ace, call Mike and see if we can link to a satellite."

"I don't really need his permission. I can just make that happen."

"I love you, you freaking geek!" yelled Gunner. "And Ace? Don't tell the girls anything right now, okay?"

"I might be a geek, but I'm not stupid. Get going."

"Let's go," said Gunner, staring at Tango, "let's bring our girls home."

CHAPTER FIVE

With Calla safe in her daddy's arms, Tango knew that they would get the vest off of her and get her to safety. Now he had to find Taylor. Running from room to room, he finally found the door to the cellar. He walked carefully, adjusting his eyes to the darkness, the twins, Eagle and Hawk, behind him.

"There," said Hawk, tapping his shoulder. In the darkness, a door was left ajar, the cold draft filtering into the damp space. He listened and heard the sounds a woman crying and took off down the tunnel.

"Fuck!" yelled Eagle. "Slow down, Tango. Don't make him do something fucking stupid. Get to the girl. We'll hold back where he can't see us. Just do you." Tango nodded at the younger man, grateful for his calm when all he could think about was killing the man holding the woman he loved.

Fucking hell, I love her. Six months of coffee and muffins, and now I figure out that I love her.

"Get up!" Javier growled at her as he pulled her hair, trying to lift her to her feet. He slapped her again, then punched her lower pelvic area, causing her to urinate herself. She cried out, doubling over again.

Oh, God, it's just like Evan all over again. Tango...

"You will fucking get up, or I will put a bullet in your brain," he said, spittle flying into her face. He pulled the tape from her mouth.

"Please, please, I can't. I'm hurting," she cried.

"Shut the fuck up and get moving," he said, yanking on her arm. When she stumbled again, he turned and slammed his fist into her face. Taylor fell back against the floor of the wet tunnel, darkness enveloping her. "Get up, cunt!"

Taylor heard him but couldn't gain any sense of what was up or down, her face filled with pain, blood oozing from her nose and mouth.

It's broken. It's broken again...

"Touch her again, and you die motherfucker," said Tango, staring down the man hovering over Taylor. "I have three guns pointed at your greasy ass. You have nowhere left to escape to. Let her go."

"You forget I hold all the cards here," he said, grinning with the switch in his hand. "You kill me. She dies."

"You kill her; we all die," said Tango, shrugging his shoulders. "Let her go, and you walk away." Javier eyed the man carefully. There weren't a lot of options here. They were truly at a standoff. If he didn't let the girl

go, he was dead either by the explosives in her vest or by one of the

bullets aimed at his head.

"How do I know you'll let me walk?" he asked, staring Tango

down.

"Because, unlike you, I have a soul and a conscience. I want the

woman to live. You've already lost the little girl. She's safe," he said,

taking another step closer. Javier took a step back, Taylor still lying at his

feet, writhing in pain, moaning.

"I don't think so," he said, smiling. He should have done what the

man asked, should have taken the deal to run. He saw it a fraction too

late, the muzzle blast of the silencer on a rifle. He saw it before he felt it.

The top of half of his hand flew into the air, the fingers instinctively

opening. Looking at the bloody palm with no fingers attached, he started

to scream, but not before a second bullet hit him square between the

eyes.

Tango rushed to scoop Taylor in his arms as she moaned against

his body, writhing in pain. She tried to push him away, but he held strong,

pulling her closer to his body.

"It's okay, honey. We've got you," he said, racing back toward the house. In the waning evening light, they noticed that her vest wasn't on a timer, and Razor made quick work of removing it as well, but it was her bloodied and battered face that gave them all pause.

Boys, you've got about three minutes to get the hell out of there before you have company.

"Let's get her to Gabi," said Gunner. "Hawk? Call Gabi and Doc. Let them know we're comin' in hot with Taylor."

Tango held onto Taylor in the backseat of the second SUV, trying to keep her from Calla's eyes. He whispered sweet things in her ear, telling her all would be okay, but the entire time hating himself for not getting to her quicker.

"You're gonna be just fine, honey. You have to be. We have a date next weekend, and I'm gonna hold you to it," he said, kissing her forehead. "Don't give up on me, Tay. Please, baby, you can't let him win."

I can't let him win again. I can't let him win...

As they pulled into the compound, Doc raced out helping Tango with Taylor.

"Get her upstairs to Gabi," he yelled, taking one look at the blood and the shape of her nose. Tango held her tightly to his chest and walked up the stairs to the medical room, lying her carefully on the table.

"I'm here, baby girl. I'm not leaving," he whispered to her. Taylor tried to open her eyes, tried to speak but just couldn't manage it. She turned toward Tango's voice, attempting to speak, but it just came out as a gurgle, blood filling her mouth.

"Turn her on her side," said Gabi. "It's okay, honey. Spit, just spit out the blood," Doc gathered a tray of instruments and started cleaning her face so Gabi could get a better idea of the damage.

"Shit!" said Gabi.

"What? What's wrong?" asked Tango in a panicked voice.

"Her nose is broken, but it's her eye socket I'm more concerned about. I think it's fractured as well. We have to get her to a trauma center. Doc? Call for an ambulance, airlift if they have it." Doc nodded, stepping outside the room. Tango could feel the tears fill his eyes, the salty liquid weeping down his cheeks.

"Hang in there, baby girl. I'm not leaving you," he whispered.

"N-not again, no more…" she said through her bloody, broken lips.

"No one will touch you again, honey, no one."

"Ambulance is coming," said Doc. "They'll get her down to the landing site, and she'll be taken by helicopter from there." Gabi nodded, continuing to attempt to staunch the bleeding as best as she could.

"Tango? I need you to step outside while I examine her pelvis," said Gabi. He shook his head.

"No, no fucking way am I leaving her," he said vehemently.

"Tango," said Doc, looking at him with a pleading expression. Tango grimaced and kissed Taylor's forehead.

"I'll be right outside, baby, not going anywhere," he said, letting the tears fall. Outside the room, he heard the murmurs of Doc and Gabi as she examined Taylor's pelvis, performing a vaginal exam as well as obtaining a urine sample. He slouched against the floor, his arms folded on his knees, his head resting against them.

He felt the hand of his friend Razor on his back.

"She'll be okay, brother. Have faith in Gabi and Doc," said Razor. Tango nodded, wiping the tears from his face.

"She... she trusted me, brother. She..." he sniffed and shook his head as Doc opened the door and nodded for him to come back inside.

"I think she has some internal damage, Tango," said Gabi. "She has swelling, bleeding both vaginally and in her urine. How long did this guy have her?"

"Five, maybe ten minutes max alone," he said.

"Shit," she muttered. "He did a lot of damage in five or ten minutes. He obviously knew how to inflict the most pain in a short period of time. I'm worried about her internal injuries. That ambulance..." Gabi stopped, hearing the sirens outside.

"Let's get her down there," said Doc, looking at Tango. "Carefully, Tango, like a box of dynamite." Tango nodded, gently lifting her from the bed and carrying her downstairs.

Tango passed the meeting room where his brothers were all seated, Doc stopping to let them know what was happening. Looking up, they spotted Doc, his shirt bloody.

"Jesus," whispered Gunner. "H-how is she?"

"She's a fucking mess. I don't know how he did so much damage in such a short period of time. Her nose is broken, a few teeth knocked out, fractured eye socket, broken wrist, broken ribs, and her pelvis is bruised along with her bladder and uterus. Angel eyes was fucking awesome in there, but she's going to need some reconstructive surgery."

"What can we do?" asked Ghost.

"Nothin' right now. Gabi called for an ambulance to move her to a hospital. She needs to be under the care of a plastic surgeon and potentially a gynecologist. We spoke, and she's agreed to tell them she was in an automobile wreck, and we found her." Ghost nodded but hated like fuck that she was put in that position.

Hearing the sounds of the ambulance, they rushed out to greet it, helping to bring Taylor down the stairs. Tango refused to leave her side, holding her hand the entire way.

"I'm going with her," he said to Ghost, who only nodded.

"Call us as soon as you know anything," he said quietly. Tango nodded, stepping into the back of the ambulance, latching onto her unbroken hand once again. They watched as it pulled out, lights and sirens going, concern for Taylor filling their minds, but right along with it were concerns for their brother.

CHAPTER SIX

"You did a good job, Dr. Slater," said the plastic surgeon, standing over Taylor's bed. Gabi nodded her silent thanks, still holding onto Taylor's hand. It had been five days of surgeries, x-rays, blood tests, MRIs, more surgery, and more tests. Now she was lying here wishing she could leave.

"Her nose will heal fine, as will the eye socket. She shouldn't have any issues with vision. The ribs will heal as well, but we're concerned about the damage done to her pelvis. Was she raped?"

"She is right here," said Taylor through her torn lips. "I wasn't raped, not today." The doctor looked up at Gabi, who gave him a look that said she had no clue what that meant.

"Honey, what do you mean not today?" asked Gabi.

"I was kidnapped and raped, beaten repeatedly for three days almost twenty years ago. He did some internal damage at that time. They were unsure if I'd ever be able to have children. My periods are erratic. I have endometriosis from the trauma, and I get frequent bladder infections."

She recited it all as if she were just telling a story to someone. Gabi's chest tightened for the pain this poor woman must have endured. Then her thoughts went to Tango, patiently waiting in the hallway, not knowing any of this.

"Did you get counseling at the time?" asked Gabi. Taylor shook her head. "Will you speak with Bree, honey?" Taylor nodded. Gabi stepped outside the room, Tango standing with his arms crossed over his chest, not-so-patiently waiting.

"How is she?" he asked, standing up straight, suddenly looking very nervous.

"She is hurt, honey, bad. She's going to need some long-term care for some of her wounds, therapy for the broken hand. She... she's going to talk to Bree." Tango nodded, biting his lower lip. Behind Gabi, the plastic surgeon walked out.

"Can I see her?" he asked.

"For a few minutes, but then let her rest," he said. Tango nodded, heading to the door. Before he could open it, Gabi touched his arm.

"Be patient with her, Tango. There are things. Things she needs to tell you," she said. Tango nodded, confused by Gabi's statement. He opened the door to see the halo of blonde curls he'd come to love. Nothing else resembled the beautiful woman he'd learned to love, though, nothing. Her face was covered in bruises, grotesquely swollen and deformed. Her eyes opened a crack, and he saw the tears sliding down.

"Don't cry, baby girl. Please don't cry," he said, sitting next to her, reaching for her unbroken hand. "It will all be okay. I'm here for you. I... I'm so damned sorry, Taylor. I should have gotten there sooner. I should have brought you to the club. I..." She held up her broken hand and shook her head slowly.

"It's... it's not your fault. N-nothing you could have done. You saved me. You saved Calla. Th-this will heal." She said quietly. He nodded, then kissed the back of her hand.

"What do you need? What can I get for you? Anything, honey, anything at all?" She stared at his beautiful face, those brown eyes staring into her soul as if reading every thought. Except he couldn't read her thoughts, couldn't see the ugliness that stained her soul, her heart. He deserved to know all her secrets. He had a right to know why she would never be the right woman for him.

"Y-you need to hear a story," she said, staring at the ceiling. Tango could only nod as she started to speak. It felt like hours. Hours of hearing torture and pain. Hours of hearing her deepest secret spilled on the ghastly white sheet beneath her broken body. His stomach threatened to spill its contents, his heart cracking with every spoken word.

"I may never be able to have children. I-I don't know."

"Honey, none of that matters, none of it. You're here now, alive, and I'm not leaving you," he said through unshed tears. She could only nod.

"Can... c-can I have some time alone? I need to talk to Bree. Get my head on straight?" she said.

"Baby girl, you can have all the time you need, but two things. One, I'm not going anywhere, and two, your head is on straight, baby. You just need to talk to someone that will help you understand that, okay?" She nodded again as he stood and kissed her forehead. She was already asleep when he lifted his lips, but it didn't stop him from saying the words.

"I love you."

CHAPTER SEVEN

By the Fourth of July, Taylor was given clearance to go home. Tango waited patiently while the nurse helped her get dressed. Her face was still swollen, black and blue, but he was starting to see glimpses of the woman he knew. Her blue eyes were a duller shade of blue, and that made his heart ache; he wanted nothing more than to bring back the brightness to those eyes.

When the door opened and the nurse exited, she touched his arm and smiled.

"Be patient with her, honey. She's been through more than most women could survive."

"I know. I plan on being patient for the rest of our lives," he said calmly.

And he meant it. He meant it more than anything else in the world. He'd spent the last two days preparing his guest room for her, although he knew she would be more comfortable at the barn for now. Eventually, he would ask her to move in, but until then, he was prepared to be patient and wait on her at the barn.

He walked into the room to find her seated in the chair. She looked up and attempted a small smile but couldn't quite manage it.

"You ready, beautiful?" he said, smiling.

"Not beautiful," she whispered, "but ready when you are. I need to get home."

"Honey, I don't think you should be alone right now. You're gonna need help showering and changing your dressings, just an extra pair of hands. I have an extra room..."

Her expression looked panicked, and Tango immediately held up his hands, taking a step back.

"Okay, no room at my house. Ghost has made one of the suites available at the barn. You'll have Gabi, Darby, Grace, and Bree close by, baby. Let us do this for you. Let me do this for you, okay?" She nodded, but he knew she wasn't completely sold on the whole idea.

Getting her to the barn, he knew she wouldn't want everyone to see her, and there were twice as many people hanging around for the big party and celebration.

"Wh-why are there so many..." she gasped.

"Relax, baby girl. Gunner and Darby got married. His whole family is here, and there are some old friends staying here as well. You don't have to see any of them, baby. I'm gonna take you up the back stairs and get you settled, okay?" She nodded, relief flooding her delicate features, and Tango wanted to slam his hand through a wall.

Opening the door, he set her bag inside and gently grasped her elbow. She was so fucking tiny next to him. Barely five-foot-two, maybe a hundred and ten pounds, her delicate bones so small beneath his big hand. Her features, when not swollen, were almost elf-like. Her huge blue eyes set against a freckled face, her pouty pink mouth below a delicate nose. She was curvy but in a small, petite way. Her breasts were small, her legs lean beneath narrow hips.

Everything about this woman set Tango on fire, everything. Seeing her tiny body next to his, this close, his protective instincts seemed in overdrive; he was ready to stand guard outside her door all night if need be. He wanted to lock her up and never let anyone near her again.

"Th-this is nice," she said, looking up at him. He nodded.

"There's a bathroom over there with a stand-up shower, but if you want a hot bath, you could always use my house – not to stay, honey

– I know. I'll go get you something to drink and some food." She shook her head.

"I-I really just want to rest, if that's okay?" He nodded, closing the door to head downstairs and congratulate Gunner and Darby. Seeing his friend look so happy was bittersweet for Tango. He wanted that happiness; he wanted the woman by his side, married. He wanted the woman who was lying upstairs alone.

"Hey, man, how is she?" asked Gunner.

"Same. I got her settled upstairs near my room, but she doesn't really want to see me." Tango shrugged his shoulders as if it didn't bother him, but Gunner knew that it damned sure did.

"She'll get there, brother. Give her time." He nodded. Tango tried to mingle with the people, talk to his brothers, but his thoughts kept returning to Taylor. Finally giving up, he turned back to the barn to head to his own room so that he could be close if she needed him. He stopped outside Taylor's room and knocked softly.

"Come in," came the meek voice.

"I was just making sure everything was okay. Do you need anything?" he asked, keeping his distance. Her face was swollen and black and blue, the features vastly different from what he remembered on the woman.

"No, no, it's okay, Tango. Tango, Tyler, why are you doing this? This wasn't your fault; you don't owe me anything."

"Not about owing shit, honey. It's about not protecting you when I should have. This is my fault, and I should have been there." She shook her head from side to side slowly, careful not to move too quickly.

"Not your fault," she said.

"It is, and every time I look at you, I see the mistakes I made. I can't stand it. It nearly kills me." Taylor felt the tears in her eyes and turned away.

"I'm tired. I think I want to be alone now," she said. He nodded, closed the door, and went across the hall to his own room. She deserved whatever she wanted as far as he was concerned. If she wanted peace and quiet, he would give it to her. If she wanted a new house, he'd buy it for her. He was already working on getting the shop back up and running.

He would give her anything she wanted.

CHAPTER EIGHT

Tango woke the next morning knowing what he needed to do. Even if Taylor didn't want it, he was going to let her know where he stood, that he loved her and wanted her in his life. He knew she wasn't ready for commitments, but he damned sure knew that he was committing to her, and she would know it.

He dressed quickly, pulling on a pair of jeans and a t-shirt. He knew the others were probably already downstairs celebrating the morning after the wedding and the continued long weekend. Stopping at her door, he knocked quietly. When there was no response, he assumed she was either still asleep or downstairs.

The noise was nearly deafening at the breakfast table. He watched as George delicately told Calla she could not bring Bullitt into the kitchen, which made her demand breakfast on the porch through tears that nearly killed poor old George. Her Uncle Hunter was relegated to the space beside her for giving her the suggestion that Bullitt should enjoy breakfast with her.

Tango walked in, looking around to see if Taylor decided to come down for breakfast, disappointment showing on his face when he didn't see her.

"I'll go check on her, Tango," said Gabi, smiling at him, patting his arm as she walked by him. He nodded his thanks as the woman disappeared upstairs. Gunner's sister-in-law was holding one of the twins, marveling at how big they were, feeling sorry for poor Gabi. Zulu could only nod and shrug. It wasn't his fault he was so damned big. Besides, Gabi wasn't exactly petite. It was her fault too.

"Tango," said Gabi, standing in the doorway, "she's gone. Sh-she left you a note." Tango swallowed hard, looking around the room at the shocked faces.

"Read it," he said quietly. "Please." Gabi nodded.

Tyler – you were right—looking at me must be very difficult for you. You don't owe me anything. You saved me and saved Calla. You should be so proud of yourself. I'm going away for a while. I need to go away for a while. I'll be selling the business, so I might not ever be back. My only regret is I wish we had our date, Tyler. I was really looking forward to finally kissing you, the only man I ever willingly wanted to kiss, desired to kiss. You deserve to be happy. Find someone you can look at and feel happiness. Yours – Tay

"Fuck," he whispered. "She thought I couldn't look at her because of her injuries. I have to find her. I have to…" Ace poked his head in the door and smiled.

"Found her." Tango turned to see the smirk on Ace's face, waiting to hear his news. "Oh, I hooked one of the trackers to her purse. Ummm, I sort of did it without asking."

"I don't give a fuck," said Tango. "I'd kiss you if I didn't think it would make you run. Where is she? Tell me!"

He followed Ace to his computer room and nodded as the man told him where she was headed. He agreed to keep lines open, so he could tell him when she stopped. Tango ran toward his bike, then thinking better of it, knowing Taylor couldn't ride, he took off in his truck.

Tango couldn't believe she'd walked out on them. What the hell was she thinking, running like that? She was in pain and couldn't drive, so she had to have called for a ride. He drove in the direction that Ace told him she was located, eyeing the small little houses with their perfectly manicured lawns and flower beds. At the end of the cul-de-sac, he saw the yellow cab idling in the driveway. Stepping out of his truck, he ran toward the taxi.

"You waiting for a blonde girl with bad bruises on her face?" he asked. The man looked him up and down, sneering.

"You hurt that little girl?" he asked.

"NO! Fuck no, I'm in love with her!" The man looked as though he didn't believe him, sneering again. "Listen, she's the love my life. I didn't hurt her. I need to protect her. Here, a hundred bucks for you to go." The man took the money and nodded.

Tango watched the cab pull away and wiped his hands on the front of his jeans. Walking toward the door, he knocked softly. He waited not-so-patiently, hearing movement behind the door. A few minutes later, the door cracked open.

"I'm almost done," she gasped. "Tango, what, why?"

"Because I'm in love with you, Taylor. You misunderstood me. I didn't mean I couldn't look at your face because of the damage. I meant I couldn't look at it and not see all the things I did wrong. It's because of me you look like that, honey. It's because of me you're in pain." Taylor felt the tears come and couldn't stop them. Tango pulled her into his body, holding her gently so as not to hurt her.

"My sweet, sweet girl. You're killing me, Tay. I love you, honey, love you so much. Why'd you run?"

"Oh, Tango, how can you love me? You know, you know what my stepbrother did. I'm broken. I'm so broken," she sobbed.

"We're all broken, honey. Some of us are broken in big pieces, easy to put back together. Others have a million little pieces that take time to be put back together. Doesn't matter to me which you are. I want to be there for you, Taylor, help you. Please don't turn me away, please."

"You said you love me. How?" Tango laughed and kissed her lips gently.

"I have no idea how, my love. All I know is it happened, and I'm not letting you go, Taylor. I can't, baby. I just would die." He held her while she cried in his arms, rubbing soft, lazy circles on her back. "Come back with me. You don't have to stay in the barn. Stay in my house. Please."

"Okay," she nodded. "Okay, Tango, but listen to me, listen." He nodded.

"I'm always listening, Taylor, always hear what you say, baby."

"Tango, I can't think when you look at me like that." He smiled at her gently, kissing the tip of her nose. "I-I will stay with you, Tango. I will stay for a few reasons."

"I'm listening, baby girl," he said, rocking her in his arms.

"One, you're right. I need help to do almost everything right now." He nodded. "Two, I have no clue what to do with the shop."

"It's being repaired as we speak, honey."

"Wh-what?" she said, looking up at him.

"I contacted your insurance provider and got Grant Zimmerman and his crew in to start the work. It's gonna take about a month, but I figure by then you might be ready to go back to work."

"I can't believe you did that for me," she whispered against his chest.

"I'd do anything for you, baby girl, anything," he said, kissing the top of her head. "Is that it? Is that all your reasons?"

"N-no. I'm scared. Terrified is the better word, Tango. Not just because of what happened here."

"Why, baby?" he said, frowning.

"M-my stepbrother, he's up for parole and may get it. Fifty, no, forty-three days now. I-I don't know what I'll do if he gets out, Tango," she shook her head from side to side. "I can't sleep. I can't breathe, knowing he's still out there."

Tango pulled her in as tightly as he dared, kissed her head again, and then pulled her back to stare up at him.

"Do you trust me, Taylor?"

"With my life," she whispered. He nodded.

"Then that's all I need to hear. You need help with your bags?" She nodded with a small grin.

"I don't know what I was thinking," she said, opening the door wider. "I told the taxi to wait while I did this, but it was going to take me hours to get what I needed. I can't lift anything. I'm down to one hand, and I can hardly breathe."

"Sit," he said, pointing her to a chair in her bedroom. "Tell me what you need."

"The suitcases are in the closet," she said, pointing. "I-I need everything. I don't spend a lot of money on clothes, so it's just jeans, sweaters, and t-shirts mostly. If you'll grab as many as the cases will hold, that would be good, and pajamas, second drawer down." He did as he was told, and she smiled as he held things up, and she said yea or nay.

"Bras and panties?" he asked. Taylor flushed a bright red, and he grinned. "Okay with me if you don't wanna wear any, honey, but I suspect you'll want some."

"Y-yes, they're in the top drawer. Is this too weird?" she asked, blushing again.

"Baby girl, me touching your panties and bras has been a fantasy of mine. Not exactly like this, but right now, I won't be picky. I'm just so fucking happy you're coming home with me, Taylor." He closed the suitcase and grabbed her hand.

"Th-thank you for coming after me, Tyler, Tango," she said.

"Tyler to you, baby girl. To you, I'm Tyler, and you don't have to thank me for doing what's natural, honey. I protect those I love, simple as that." She let out a long slow breath, and he grinned, knowing she was still feeling uncertain.

"You ready to go home?" he asked without thinking.

"I'm ready to go to *your* home, Tyler, but yes, I'm ready."

"Good enough for me, baby girl. Good enough for now."

CHAPTER NINE

By the time Tango got her settled into his home, she was exhausted once again. He put her to bed – in her bed – then texted the team to let them know she was safe. He also casually mentioned the issue with her stepbrother and his possible parole. As predicted, exactly four minutes later, the precise amount of time it takes to walk from the barn to his home, all of his brothers were at his door.

"Come in," he said quietly. "She's sleeping, so why don't we go out back." They stepped through the French doors to his patio, finding a seat amongst the custom-made outdoor furniture. Tango was good with his hands, not just machines but woodworking as well, and he'd made a huge custom outdoor set when he built the house. Winter, summer, spring, or fall, he was going to enjoy the outdoors.

"What did you mean her stepbrother is getting out?" asked Razor.

"He's up for parole, and she seems to think he's going to get it. Maybe we can get Kat to look into this," he said, looking at Whiskey.

"I know she will, brother, but you know that if we start looking into it, you're going to find out all the horrid details of her kidnapping."

"I know," he said, nodding. "She told me everything, or at least I think it was everything she could remember. It was fucking brutal. Beyond. All I could think about were those little girls..."

The men seated around him nodded, all either having been there or heard the story a number of times.

"Do you need me to cover at the garage?" asked Razor.

"Thanks, brother. I don't think full-time. Maybe just be flexible with me for a while. I want to make sure she knows I'm literally just across the yard."

"What do you need from a security standpoint?" asked Ghost.

"Nothing right now," he said, looking down at his feet. "I have the system all of you have on the house. I'll get her a tracker for her body instead of her purse. The shop won't be reopened for at least a month, and she wouldn't want to go there anyway right now. I think if I can just get her healthy, continue her sessions with Bree, that's all I can do right now."

"She yours, brother?" asked Whiskey. Tango nodded, a somber expression on his face.

"Knew it weeks ago and was too damned afraid to tell her. If I had… if only…"

"Can't do that to yourself, brother," said Razor. "Can't do the if only or what if. You'll kill yourself, and right now, that girl needs you. Focus on now, brother." Tango nodded, and they relaxed into an easy conversation. He heard the door open, and Taylor stepped out, looking slightly well-rested.

"There she is," smiled Razor. "How you feeling, honey?"

"I'm good, R-Razor, right?" she asked.

"That's right, honey, or you can call me Diego, either works." She gave him a tentative smile, and Tango stood to give her his seat.

"Need a pain pill, baby?" he asked. Taylor blushed at his use of such an intimate term in front of his friends.

"No, I'm tired of sleeping and taking them. They make me feel awful, and they remind me of…" She swallowed, looking up at the men, their expressions suddenly possessive and angry. "You all know?"

"We know some, honey, not all," said Ghost. "He won't get to you here, Taylor." She nodded and then took a deep breath.

"That's what they said when I was in the hospital, but he did."

"What do you mean?" asked Hawk.

"They had him in custody awaiting trial. I was hospitalized for almost a month. The damage…"

"Baby girl, you don't have to tell us that if you don't want to," said Tango, taking her hand.

"The damage wasn't just on the outside. It was on the inside too. I wasn't alert, wasn't conscious through most of it. Sort of a blessing in disguise, really, but nevertheless, I woke to find out that there was a lot of internal damage.

"My stepfather, my stepfather knew that his son wasn't right in the head but never told my mom or me. Evan had been abusing and killing animals since he was ten. When his dad started dating my mom, he spoke about Evan all the time but never brought him around me. He just kept saying he would be a good big brother.

"When they finally decided to get married, I met Evan the night before the wedding. I was thirteen, and he was seventeen. He cornered me and kissed me hard. I'd never been kissed by a boy, so I was more than a little shocked. When I told my mother, she said she was certain it was just him showing he would be a protective brother."

"Fucking hell," growled Eagle.

"Yea, my personal hell. I learned quickly to lock the bathroom door or my bedroom door. He had no boundaries at all. He would rub against me any chance he got, but at school, he was mean to me, acting like he hated me. Every time I tried to say something to my parents, they would just dismiss it, so I learned to not say anything. I know now that made Evan think I liked it.

"The weekend, the weekend he took me, he'd just turned eighteen, and I was fourteen. I woke to find my parents gone for a long weekend. They left Evan in charge of me."

"Jesus, honey," said Razor, swallowing hard.

"Yea, I prayed to Jesus a lot that weekend. I was obviously a virgin, totally inexperienced, and sheltered. I was… am… small. Evan was much bigger. Not as big as you guys, but he obviously outweighed me and was much stronger. I-I just couldn't fight back."

"We can teach you, honey," said Zulu, "to fight back. I can teach you some self-defense."

"Y-you would do that?" she asked, shocked.

"Honey, we'd do just about anything to protect family, and as of this morning, I do believe you have become permanent family around here," grinned Ghost.

"Thank you. I don't think you need the details of the attack, but what followed is important. He was being transferred from county lock-up and attacked the guard, breaking free. I woke up the next morning with him standing over me in the hospital. I was so stunned I couldn't speak... couldn't move. He didn't touch me... he just stared at me and said, 'we're not done.' The police swarmed into the room and took him away."

"Jesus, baby girl," said Tango, kissing her head. "That must have been awful." She shook her head.

"The awful part was in the courtroom when he tried to make it look like I wanted it, that I wore skimpy clothes or my cheerleading uniform around the house to get his attention. His lawyer peppered me with accusations and questions, saying I did it intentionally to get him to notice me, to get him to teach me the ways of the world." She gave an undignified snort and looked away for a minute, brushing her tears away.

"He took the stand for himself and said I begged him that morning. Begged him. Told the courtroom that I liked the pain. I took the stand and defended myself as best I could, but in all of that, my parents, my mother and my stepfather never once came to my defense. Not once. They never spoke up and told the court how I had gone to them complaining of his behavior, about the kiss the night before the wedding. Nothing. They said nothing. They let me be humiliated in that courtroom staring down the man who'd destroyed me, except I wasn't going to let that happen. Now, now, he's going to be out there again. He's going to be free, and I'll be living my life in fear once again."

There was silence around the patio, several of the men looking in the other direction, and Taylor knew their emotions were bubbling to the surface quickly.

"I'm sorry if I said too much," she whispered.

"Never be sorry, Taylor," said Zulu. "Never."

"We're going to make sure you're safe. Even if your stepbrother gets out, we'll handle it," said Razor. "Where is he now?"

"Eastern Pennsylvania Correctional. He's in general population, and his attorneys are arguing that he's been a 'model' prisoner. He got his college degree; he's been a tutor for other prisoners; he's even done some work with animals. God, he used to torture and kill animals. I mean, I want to believe in rehabilitation, but they didn't see the monster I did!"

"Let us check into all of this, honey," said Razor. "You just get well, okay?" She nodded, slowly standing and moving toward the house.

"I'm kind of hungry. Can I fix some dinner?" she asked.

"You don't cook until you're well," said Tango, smiling. "We can either eat with the rest of the team at the barn, or we can eat here, just you and me."

"I-I don't want to scare Calla. She was so frightened in that van..."

"Say no more, honey. We'll eat here until you're feeling more like yourself." She nodded and walked inside, then turned to face the men.

"I know you know what you're doing. I mean, I know a little about the Steel Patriots and what you do, but don't get hurt for me, please." She asked pleadingly.

She closed the door, and Tango saw her head go back down the hallway to the bedroom. Letting out a long slow breath, he finally released his fisted fingers and flexed them back and forth.

"I'm going to kill her stepbrother. I just want you all to know that now." The rest of them nodded.

"Fine by me," said Ghost. "Just let us have some fun with him before you do."

CHAPTER TEN

Tango tossed the salad, keeping his eye on the soup as he did. He knew that Taylor would have difficulty chewing anything, so he made sure that all of their meals were easy to eat, easy to chew. It turns out it was good for him as he'd lost about four pounds of fat with cutting down on the meat he was eating.

"It smells good," she said from behind him. He turned to see the Taylor from before, her pert little nose healed and perfect for her face, the bruising gone, her teeth replaced. She looked freshly showered and clean, the little khaki shorts showing off her lean legs.

"You look beautiful," he said, staring at her. She blushed, looking down, and then looked toward the patio.

"It's... it's cooler this evening. Maybe we can eat outside," she said. He nodded, grinning at her. It was now early August, and in their little mountain community, that meant warm days and cool nights, something Tango loved.

"I was thinking," he said, smiling at her, "maybe I could take you out on the bike tomorrow." She looked at him wide-eyed and smiled.

"Really? You'd let me ride with you?" He laughed.

"Why wouldn't I, baby girl? You're my girl, Taylor. I know you're still struggling with that, but you're mine." She stared at him, trying to decide if he was telling the truth or not.

"I'd like to go for a ride with you tomorrow. I'd like to be your girl," she said quietly. "I-I haven't dated much, Tyler, like at all, really. I mean, I had a few dates in college, but it wasn't anything, and then a few when I moved here permanently, but nothing really. I guess what I'm trying to tell you, to warn you, is I haven't been with anyone since what happened."

"Ever?" he said, looking surprised.

"Never."

"Thank you for telling me, baby. Everything moves at your pace, Taylor. Everything. I want you in every way a man could want a woman, and I do mean every way, but I also know you need time." She nodded and moved around the counter, wrapping her arms around his waist.

"M-maybe I could start by sleeping in your bed tonight?" she said against his chest. "Not... not sex... just... I want to lay next to you if that's okay."

"Honey, that is more than okay with me, if you're sure. I don't want you to feel like you have to."

"No," she said, shaking her head. "I've been thinking about it for weeks now. I get scared in the bedroom alone. I hear a noise and jump. I know that sounds clingy, but I just want to be close to you, to feel you next to me. Can we do that?"

"We can so do that, baby girl," he said, kissing her again.

He'd been living with her for weeks now, doing nothing more than a peck here or soft kiss there. He held her; he hugged her; he touched her with clothing on, but nothing else. Now as he pulled away, she pulled his head down toward her. Carefully leaning forward, allowing her to take the lead, she pressed her lips more firmly against his, gently exploring the seam of his lips.

"Y-you're so tall," she whispered. He nodded and then lifted her to sit on the counter, spreading her legs wide so he could fit between them. She smiled. "Better."

Tango thought he would explode in his shorts at the simple touch of her hands on his face. Her lips were soft and tasted like strawberries.

Her delicate fingers danced across his jaw and between their mouths, gliding along his lower lip.

"You taste so good," she said, staring at him.

"Baby girl, you have no idea what you do to me. I've been dreaming of that kiss for months now."

"Months?"

"Months, honey. I have a secret to tell you, Taylor. I don't really like muffins," he said, grinning.

"Wh-what? But, but you came into the shop at least three times a week for coffee and a muffin! Why wouldn't you tell me?"

"Because I wasn't coming in for the muffin, honey, I was coming in so I could see you, talk to you, just get to know you. You were so damned shy, and I have to admit, I wasn't much better around you. I've never had trouble talking to women before, but around you, I just couldn't find my words. It's how I knew, baby girl. It's how I knew you were it."

"I can't believe you came in all those days eating a muffin. I mean, you could have at least eaten a cupcake or something," she said, grinning at him.

"Yea," he laughed, "I suppose I could have. Truth is, baby girl, I would have eaten pigs' feet just to spend a few minutes in your company."

"Tyler, kiss me again," she said, smiling.

"Gladly, but just to be clear, you kissed me."

She started to protest, but he took her mouth more fiercely, covering her beautiful lips with his own, tasting her. Taylor scooted closer to the edge of the counter, his groin pressed against her warm core. She felt his length and hardness and nearly gasped out of shock and fear, memories flooding her. Except this wasn't Evan. This was Tango, and he was being patient and kind. He was controlling himself as a man would do, simply kissing her.

Taylor wasn't sure where her courage came from, but she grabbed one of his big, rough, callused hands and pressed it to her breast. He let his hand just stay there for a minute and then began softly kneading her breasts. She let out a long slow sigh against his lips as he pulled back, staring at her.

"You're the most beautiful woman I've ever known," he said, kissing her. "I want this, baby girl. I want you, but I think maybe you need to slow down." She looked into his eyes, at first hurt, and then realized he was showing restraint by giving her the choice to back off a bit. Nodding, she bit her lower lip, looking away.

"Taylor, look at me, baby girl. I want this so bad, honey. This bad," he said, taking her tiny hand and laying it against his thick, hard length. "But I love you enough to wait and let this be perfect. I want you to want this and be ready for it. Hear me loud and clear, baby girl. This will happen when you're ready."

"Thank you, Tyler," she said, kissing him again, her hand still resting against his cock. She rubbed her hand against him, feeling his length, her face flushing at her boldness. Tyler groaned, closing his eyes as she rubbed him through his shorts. "Does this feel good?"

"Yea, yea, baby, but if you don't stop, I'm gonna embarrass myself here." She only smiled.

"Maybe, maybe you let me touch you. I want to see and feel without you touching me. Can we do that?" she asked.

"Yea, baby girl, we can do that." He unzipped his shorts and shoved them to his ankles, his big cock bobbing free. He stood back for her to take a good long look.

"Wow, that's… it's big… and beautiful," she blushed. Tango was trying to control himself. He wanted to wrap her legs around him and dive in but knew it wasn't time. "Can I touch you?" He nodded, moving closer to her.

Taylor reached out, feeling the velvety soft skin against her fingers. She expected it to be rough like the man, but it was so soft and warm. Wrapping her fingers around him, she stroked up and down and heard him let out a long moan. His hips moved toward her, and she knew she was doing something right.

"Fuck, baby, that feels so good," he murmured.

"Like this?" she asked, moving up and down, feeling the wet drip at the tip. He could only nod. Taylor looked down to see heavy, big balls swinging back and forth. Reaching out with her other hand, she gently held them, feeling their weight in the palm of her hand.

"Oh, God, baby girl. You're gonna make me cum, honey," he said, looking at her through lust-filled eyes. Weeks of doing nothing except stroking himself was making this moment feel like a fucking wet dream. He was going to explode in her hand; she had no clue what effect she was having on him.

"Please, let me see it. Let me do this," she said pleadingly.

He nodded, laying his own hand over hers and helping her move up and down, faster, harder, stronger, his hips jutting in and out. She instinctively spread her legs wider for him, still clad in her shorts but noting that her panties were drenched. She saw the first spurt of liquid and looked down in awe as it squirted on her legs. Tyler's body jerked with satisfaction as the last bit spewed on her hand.

"Fuck, baby girl. Look at the mess I made," he said, kissing her.

She looked down at her hand and lifted it to her lips, tasting him, running his seed along her lips, and then licking. Smiling, she let a finger glide along the stream on her leg and did the same. Looking down, she noticed that Tango was already getting hard again.

"You like when I do that?" she asked innocently.

"Baby girl, I could watch you doing that all day long. That's fucking hot, and you are so damned beautiful you make me harder than I've ever been."

"I like it, all of it, and you made me wet," she said, flushing.

"I can take care of you, baby, like you did for me. Will you let me?" She nodded shyly, and he unzipped her shorts, pulling them off.

Spreading her legs wide, he kneeled in front of her, touching her opening gently, gliding his fingers along her slit.

"Stop me if you don't like it, okay?"

"I-I like it so far," she breathed.

"Eyes open, baby. Look at me so you know it's me," he said.

She looked down at him, his eyes so shiny with love and desire, his big tongue extended toward her, and she felt the heat against her sensitive skin and moaned. Oh wow, this was so much better than touching herself.

Tango let his tongue lick up and down, tasting the sweet juice of Taylor's pussy. He slid one finger into her tight hole and felt himself harden, standing erect once again. She lay one tiny hand at the back of his head, and he smiled.

"That's it, baby. Hold me there. Fuck my face, Taylor," he growled. She nodded, still looking down at him. He let two fingers slide inside her and then took the tiny nub between his teeth, sucking.

"Oh, oh, wow. Do that again. Please do that again," she said.

He nodded, going back to the task at hand. She tasted so fucking good; he wanted to bury himself inside her. If he were being the old Tango, he'd be getting rough, shoving three or four fingers inside her. Taylor was so damned tight, two was all she could do right now. He'd have to stretch her before penetrating. For now, this was heaven.

"Tyler, I'm... oh wow..."

"Take it, baby. Fuck my face," he growled.

She pushed his head further between her legs, and he lapped at her opening, sucking and plunging his fingers inside her. Crying out her release, her tiny body shook against his mouth. When she settled, he finished by licking her clean, then stood kissing her. Her eyes went wide with the taste of her body on his lips, at first uncertain if she liked it, then taking him completely by surprise when she traced her tongue over his mouth.

Still standing before her naked from the waist down, Taylor looked down to see him hard again.

"Should we do that again?" she said, smiling at him. Tango laughed, pulling her against his body, wrapping her legs around his waist as he lifted her off the counter.

"Feel that, honey?" he said, touching the tip of his cock to her opening. She nodded, biting her lip. "That's because of you. All for you when you're ready. Until then, we can do what we just did all day long, baby girl. All fucking day long."

"Good," she said, kissing him, grinding her pelvis against his velvety, hot length. "I think I want to do that again... like after dinner." Tango laughed again, holding her tighter.

"I love you, baby girl," he said against her. And then the sweetest sound ever.

"I love you too, Tyler."

CHAPTER ELEVEN

He walked toward the table, the two men in suits waiting for him patiently. They should be fucking patient. They were getting paid enough to be patient. He, however, wasn't so patient anymore. Twenty fucking years he'd been locked up. Twenty years because that little cock-tease wouldn't admit that she'd wanted him.

When his father said he was getting married again, he thought he might leave home, but when he saw that sweet little piece of ass walking in front him, he knew he was going to taste her. She was just a kid, but her little breasts were so perfect, her freckled face and blonde curls so lush. He'd kissed her at the rehearsal dinner and knew immediately that she wanted him. Young ones always tried to play innocent, always acting like they didn't know. He broke in more than a few in his short seventeen years. One was only twelve, but that little bitch already had huge tits, and she loved it when he bit down on them.

Yea, his stepsister wanted him, and he knew it. He'd set up a camera in her bedroom to watch her, and she'd put on a show for him every morning and every night, her rocking little body stripping in front of him.

couldn't seem to stop himself. He fucked her in every hole she had, making her bleed and beg for more, and the little cunt begged. Yea, she wanted him, and she would have him again. He could already feel himself getting hard just sitting there. His pants were tented by the time he sat down.

The two attorneys were a gift from someone inside, someone who only asked for his loyalty and his cock. He didn't like men, but sometimes you had to play the game to win. A few times a week, the other man would come into his cell and tell him to bend over or suck his cock or fuck him. At first, he was sickened by it. What sort of pervert fucks other men? Then he realized twenty years without a woman was more than he could take. A hole is a hole, right?

"When am I getting out?" he asked the first man.

"We're not sure, Evan. Your stepsister has a new attorney pleading her case with the parole board. They're going to give her another chance to appear before them to deny your parole."

He grimaced, slamming his fist against the table. The guard started to step forward, but the attorney raised his hand nodding the man off.

"She's playing her fucking games. She wants my dick, and she's trying to make me harder while she plays."

"Evan, I don't think your sister is playing any games. She doesn't want you, and even if you get parole, you're going to be relegated to staying in the area with an ankle monitor. Your sister, from what I understand, lives in another state." He raised his eyebrows at that news.

"What the fuck do you mean? Where is she living?" he asked.

"I don't know. We're not given that information, but you won't be allowed to leave the state. You need to continue to see the prison shrink, Evan. It will show the board that you're following recommendations." He grinned, leaning back in his chair. Gripping his still semi-hard cock through his pants, he stroked it a few times. The attorneys looked away in disgust.

"Fucking shrink wanted me too. You could tell. Yea, I'll go back to her."

"Another thing," said the man, "they found one of the dogs you were working with dead in his pen. They suspect that was you, Evan. You're going to need to answer for that." He shrugged his shoulders and grinned at the man.

"Dogs die. It's gonna happen. Just get me the fuck outta here. I was promised the best attorneys if I fucked that slimy Mexican, so get me outta here."

"I may need to remind you, Evan, that we are both Mexican, and we are paid by that slimy Mexican." He lifted his hands and smiled.

"Ooops," he grinned. His expression sobered, and he stood. "Just do your damned job and get me out of here." Turning, he walked back to the guard, who let him through to the general population.

"Sometimes I hate this job," said one of the men. "That's a man that should not get out."

"Maybe, we let Hector know how we feel." He nodded.

"Maybe, we do. Let's talk with him at our meeting next week."

CHAPTER TWELVE

The Steel Patriots Monday morning meetings were always short and sweet. A general business review on the bar, restaurant, bike shop, gym, and now the clinic. After the general review of business, Zulu opened the door to allow Kat to enter with Taylor.

"Kat, Taylor, good morning," said Ghost. "Do you have an update for us?"

"Yes, first of all, just for the record, Taylor, may I discuss everything in front of the team?" she asked.

"Of course," she nodded, her hands folded neatly in her lap. Tango reached over and threaded her fingers with his own gripping her hand tightly.

"Evan Black, as we all know, is coming up for parole. I've gotten the board to extend the hearing date to September first, but he's screaming that we're violating his rights. We have a few things on our side. One is that one of the dogs he was working with was found dead in his pen last week. The cameras were mysteriously turned off during his time in the area with the animals. He's been removed from the team that works with the dogs, but the damage is done."

"What kind of man does shit like this?" asked Hawk.

"He's not a man," said Taylor. "He's an animal, and he believes he's untouchable." Bree stepped inside the room and smiled.

"Sorry I'm late."

"Perfect timing," said Kat. "Bree, will you please tell everyone what you discovered after speaking to the prison therapist and reading the files on Evan Black." She nodded, giving a supportive smile to Taylor.

"Evan was ordered to attend therapy sessions twice a week, as well as group therapy. For the first two years, he was combative, to say the least. He fought the therapists every step of the way, even threatening them with bodily harm. Then he suddenly became a model patient. He thought he was outsmarting the therapist, but believe me, this therapist knew what he was doing."

"In his notes, he's diagnosed Evan with paranoid schizophrenia, as well as delusional tendencies and fantasies with women. He said he was the most narcissistic patient he'd ever diagnosed and refused to give up on his belief that Taylor," she stopped and looked at the other woman.

"It's okay. He believes that I wanted... that I was asking for it. I know. He said it over and over again in the courtroom."

"That is what he said, but the therapist at the prison didn't believe him. About eighteen months ago, this guy retired, and they sent in a woman."

"To an all-male prison?" asked Hawk. "What the fuck?

"That's exactly what I said," grinned Bree. "Dr. Altman is a sixty-two-year-old woman who has been a therapist and group counselor for thirty-five years. During her first encounter with Evan, he tried to get her to have sex with him."

"Holy shit," mumbled Eagle.

"Exactly. She was so uncomfortable, she refused to see him again alone. Because of that, he was granted the right to have a male therapist. There have been several going in and out since they don't have budget for another full-time person. I spoke to Dr. Altman and the warden. We have been authorized to send in someone from our team."

"No, nope, no fucking way!" said Doc, standing. "You are not going inside the prison. You're pregnant, Bree. Fuck!"

"Calm down, you overgrown alpha," she said, standing with her hands on her hips. "I'm not suggesting me. I'm suggesting we send in one of you. If we can get him to open up to one of you, find out what he's thinking, we can stop it. The therapists all say his only goal is to convince others that what he's thinking or feeling is normal. It will be awful to do, but someone will have to be an empathetic ear for him. The warden does not want this guy let loose, yet they can't just kill him."

Ghost looked at Bree and back at Doc. He sensed there was something she wasn't telling the group, and he liked having all the information before he went in on any mission.

"What else, Bree? What else is there?" asked Ghost. She nodded, smiling at him.

"Dr. Altman and the warden discovered that Evan is working with another prisoner, Hector Castro. Castro is running a small gang of Hispanics inside the prison. Within the first week, he made Evan his bitch. Over the years, he's gotten him prime jobs inside the prison, extra favors, that sort of thing. When his parole hearing was coming up, he asked Castro for a favor – new attorneys. These two attorneys fed information back to Castro, letting him know what we already knew. Evan is not right in the head."

"I'm still not following," said Whiskey.

"The warden is willing to look the other way if we can get information that will keep Evan locked up, and he believes that Castro will help us. Dr. Altman will submit the information as if she obtained it. It will be Evan's word against hers."

"Wait, she's willing to risk her license for this?" asked Ghost.

"She is. He's that sick that she's willing to do this."

"Okay, so we have a month to put someone in there and pretend to be a shrink, gather information, and then make sure Taylor gets to the parole hearing and nails this shit closed. Is that right?" asked Razor.

"That's about right," said Bree.

"I'll do it." Razor stood, looking at the other men around the table. "Listen, I have an undergraduate degree in psychology, enough to get me into trouble. I speak Spanish. I'll be able to communicate with Castro and his men if necessary, and I'm clean cut. No beard, no long hair, no tattoos."

"He's right," said Bree. "He has the look of a young professional and someone that Evan would believe he could easily manipulate."

"D-Diego, Razor," said Taylor, finally speaking, "you can't do this. There has to be another way."

"No other way, honey," he said, smiling at her. "Besides, I know what I'm doing, and keeping you safe for my brother is my honor." She shook her head, tears spilling down her cheeks.

"Okay," said Ghost, "let's make sure this shit is buttoned up. Razor, come up with an alias, and for fuck sake, don't make it Diego. Let Bree help you with all the paperwork. Ace can make it look official. Hawk and Eagle? You're going to go with him. Stay in the same hotel and make sure he goes into the prison and comes out. If he doesn't, blow that fucking place to hell."

CHAPTER THIRTEEN

"You ready, baby girl?" asked Tango.

She looked so damned cute in her jeans and cowboy boots, the flannel shirt tucked into her waist, the zippered leather jacket hugging her tiny upper body. He handed her the helmet and helped her secure it on her head. Climbing on the bike, he held out his hand to her.

"Place your feet on the pegs, here. Wrap your arms around my waist tight, tighter, honey. Good. Don't ever grab my arms or shoulders. It could cause me to swerve and wreck. If you have to stop, just tap my thigh. When the bike turns, leans, or moves, you move with it. If you're holding tight to me, pressed against my body, just lean with my body. Good?" She nodded, biting her bottom lip, and he turned slightly, smiling at her.

"You're gonna do great," he said, kissing her lips.

"I'm just nervous," she said in the microphone. "I know this is a big part of your life, and I don't want to ruin it for you."

"You won't ruin it, baby girl. If you don't like it, we'll try again. If you still don't like it, well, then we'll just figure out a compromise. Nothing says you gotta ride with me. I'd just sure love to have you wrapped around me." She nodded, and he slowly accelerated the bike toward the main road.

Snaking around the big mountain curves, at first, Taylor closed her eyes. Tango's sweet voice filtered through the helmet.

"Don't be afraid, baby girl. You're missing out on some beautiful scenery."

She opened her eyes and smiled. This wasn't so bad after all. The bike hugged the road just as Tango told her it would. The rumble between her legs was exciting and, if she were honest, stimulating. She could feel her nipples harden as the big pipes roared beneath her, her legs squeezing his thighs.

Tango reached back and gripped one of her legs, rubbing his big gloved hand up and down, feeling the power in her tiny legs against his own. She was the first woman he'd ever allowed on the back of his bike, and she would damn sure be the last. It was the hottest fucking thing he'd ever experienced, having her perfect little teacup breasts pressed against his back, her blonde curls peeking from beneath the helmet.

He suddenly realized he was riding with a raging hard-on. As if hearing his own thoughts, Taylor let one hand slide down his abs, feeling the muscles beneath her fingers, and then lower still, resting between his thighs. He gripped her hand and held it still, breathlessly speaking to her.

"I want that, baby. Just not now, not while we're moving." She blushed but nodded, grinning at him.

"Sorry, I think I'm a little turned on," she said in his ear.

That was all Tango needed to hear. Finding a narrow turn off on a dirt road, he pulled over, yanking off his helmet. Turning on the bike, he grabbed Taylor by the waist, lifting her body, and settling her in front of him, her legs wrapped around him.

"Oh!" she said in surprise.

"Tell me you're fucking turned on, and I'm gonna do something about it, baby girl," he said, tossing her helmet to the ground. He unzipped her jacket, shoving the shirt up her body. He pushed the cups of her bra aside, his mouth taking each nipple between his teeth, sucking.

"Oh God, Tyler, that's so good, honey," she said, arching her back off the gas tank.

"I want you so bad," he murmured. She nodded, unwrapping her legs. She toed off her boots and shoved her jeans down. "Taylor…"

"Shhh, before I change my mind. I want you too, Tyler."

He straddled the bike, undoing his jeans and shoving them down, his thick cock finally free from its prison. Taylor climbed back on, her legs on either side of his body, opening wide for him. His big palm flat against her stomach as his thumb rubbed her hard, little nub.

"Tyler, please, honey..."

"I'm gettin' there, baby girl. Gotta make you cum for me first." She nodded, writhing against his hand, calling his name as she finally released on his fingers. Hovering above her, he placed the tip of his cock at her perfectly wet opening, teasing her entrance.

"Slow and easy, baby. Tell me if I hurt you," she nodded again, looking down to see his big purple head resting at her lips.

"It looks so good. That big thick cock against me. It looks beautiful," she whispered.

"Yea, it fucking does," he groaned, pushing forward just a bit. She was so fucking tight; she was strangling his dick. "Fucking hell, baby girl..."

"Don't... don't stop. You feel so good, Tyler, please, more..."

He nodded, pushing in further, her breasts gleaming in the sunlight, her body arched off the bike, rising to greet him. She looked like the cover of a biker magazine, all lean arms and legs, molding to the tank of the bike. Tango moved closer, driving in a little deeper, and she gasped.

He stilled, worried that he'd hurt her. Fucking sure she was probably gonna bleed. Nodding at him, he kissed her and thrust all the way inside her as she gasped against his lips.

"Breathe, baby girl," he said, whispering in her ear, her pussy literally fitting around the skin of his dick. "Just breathe. Oh fuck, you feel good..."

"Tyler, honey, you're so big, so perfect," she moaned like a fucking sex goddess, and his dick grew bigger. "Fuck me, Tyler, please."

He couldn't help his own animal instincts as he moved, faster and faster, driving inside her tight little hole. He was focused on keeping the bike balanced, keeping her legs wrapped around him, keeping his dick inside her, and making her cum. This was an exercise in multi-tasking.

"Tyler, I'm cumming, Tyler!" she screamed.

"Do it. Fucking do it!" he yelled back at her.

Her little body shuddered beneath him, shaking with the orgasm racking her body. He was right behind her, his big cock draining inside her, filling her to the brim and then some, leaking down that perfectly pale crack of her ass.

Tango leaned forward, kissing her nipples, working his way up her body to find her lips and take her mouth, almost violently. He was surprised when she followed his lead, gripping his head and devouring his mouth. His dick was still buried inside her when she started to move again.

"More, I want more, Tyler," she moaned.

He stepped off the bike, her legs still wrapped around him. Setting her feet on the ground, he turned her to lean over the bike, her cute little ass facing him. Kneeling down, he buried his face in her pussy, lapping up their juices, only to replace it with more. Standing, he slid inside her, her muscles contracting around him, sending him into dizzying bliss.

"Fuck, baby girl, that pussy is made for me," he growled. She nodded, wiggling against him, swirling her little ass in tiny circles. Tango gripped her waist, thrusting against her. "Play with yourself, honey, cum for me."

Taylor nodded, rubbing her fingers against herself, relishing in the feel of Tango filling her up. It only took seconds for her to explode again, and he followed, filling her up once more. Tango pulled her flush against his chest, his big hands hovering over her sensitive breasts as she moaned.

"Baby girl, that was the hottest fucking thing I've ever experienced. Remind me to take you on a ride at least once a day," he growled in her ear. She wiggled her little ass against his semi-hard cock, reaching behind her, grabbing his neck. He leaned down, kissing her face.

"You've created a monster, Tyler. I want more, again. I need you inside me, honey."

"Fuuuckk, yea, baby girl." He pulled off his jacket and lay his and hers on the ground, then, kneeling, took her from behind, slamming into her, his balls slapping against that beautiful pink pussy of hers. He wanted this woman so bad; he came over and over again, his body shaking with need and desire.

It was nearly two hours later when they finally got up from the ground. Taylor picked up their jackets, brushed them off, and noticed the stains of their lovemaking on the lining.

"I guess we need to get these cleaned," she said, blushing.

"Nope," he said, kissing her. "Every time I put this jacket on, I'm gonna see those cum stains and remember this. Hottest fucking thing ever, baby girl." He pulled her in for another kiss, lightly slapping her ass, and she laughed.

"Take me home, Tyler. I want to fuck you in our bed."

"Our bed?" he grinned.

"That's right, our bed," she smiled. "I'm not going to fight this anymore, Tyler. I love you, and I don't want to leave. Take me home... to our home... make love to me."

"Baby girl, we didn't use any protection," he said, kissing her. "I know they said you might not be able to have children, but if you can, we damned sure just made some."

She nodded at him, a sad smile covering her lips.

"Hey, hey, baby, I'd be happy either way. If you get pregnant, great. If not, and we decide we want children, we'll adopt. Okay?"

"Okay," she said, kissing him. "Now, bed."

"Yes, ma'am!"

CHAPTER FOURTEEN

Although the renovations on the coffee shop were complete, and she could re-open at any time, Taylor didn't feel as though she could go back to work yet. She felt safe and secure behind the gates of the Steel Patriots, and until she was certain her stepbrother would never see the light of day again, she was staying close to home.

She soon discovered the advantages of working just a few minutes from home, when every day at lunch, Tango walked in ready for his lunch – usually her. Taylor learned quickly to have a sandwich ready for him to take on his way out because he usually spent the entire time burled inside her.

Most of her day was spent rearranging her own furnishings inside the house they now shared, having put her tiny little cottage up for sale. She realized that Tyler was only picky about two things, his motorcycle and the cleanliness of the bathroom. Fortunately, she was a bit of a neat freak, so the house was always perfectly clean when he arrived home.

The other wives quickly enveloped her into their family, and Taylor found herself spending a lot of time visiting with Gabi and the twins, Grace and JT, as well as the precocious Calla. Careful not to fall into the funk she sometimes did when she was around children for too long, she learned that it was okay to yearn for a child.

"You okay, honey?" asked Gabi.

"Yeah, yeah, good, really." Gabi looked at her, not believing her, and smiled. "I just... I was wondering if you could tell me whether or not you think I can have children?" Gabi nodded.

"I can, honey, but your obstetrician might be the better person." Gabi noticed her disappointed look and conceded. "I tell you what, let's walk over to the clinic and take a look. I can do a sonogram of your uterus and see what's going on, if anything."

"You don't mind?" she asked.

"Not at all, honey, but I want you to be prepared for the positive or negative, okay? Even if you can't carry, there are other options, Taylor." She nodded, following Gabi to the clinic. They passed the garage, but she didn't really want to let Tango know what she was doing yet. The clinic was relatively empty except for Bree seeing patients on her side. Gabi led her to the treatment room and prepped her.

"Okay, let's see what we have, honey." She slid the cold wand inside her vagina, speaking to her in a soothing voice. "Good girl, the hard part is done. Okay, hmmm, I do see some endometriosis, but that can be lasered away. Your uterus looks fine. There is some small residual scarring, but nothing that would indicate to me that you couldn't carry a child. Push back, honey."

"I think we should get some blood work and check your hormone levels. I want to get you to someone who can take care of the endo, and then you can go from there. Do you want to try for a baby, Taylor?"

"I-I don't know, honestly, maybe. I mean, I see all the babies around here, and it's as if my womb is calling out to me." Gabi nodded, laughing at the young woman. "Gabi? Is there any way you can take care of all this? I don't want to see anyone else."

"I can do it for you, honey. I'll get Doc to get everything we need, and we'll schedule it. You'll need to let Tango know. You won't be able to have sex for about ten days after the procedure." She nodded, nibbling on her lower lip.

"He's been so sweet, so kind, and patient." Gabi nodded, not saying anything to allow the woman enough time to gather her thoughts. "He didn't touch me at all for the first three weeks. Then when I finally gave the nod, he let me control everything. Then... then it was just him lying in bed at night holding me. It had to have been hard for him, literally." She laughed, and Gabi laughed with her.

"He never once forced himself on me. Not once. When I was finally ready. Damn, I was ready," she smiled.

"I know what you mean," said Gabi. "I waited fifteen years for Quin. We met briefly after I operated on him, and then he didn't remember the encounter but dreamed about it. I remembered everything. When we finally reconnected, damn, girl, it was like lightning in a bottle. I just wanted to jump his bones. We married within two weeks."

"Wow! That's definitely fast."

"Taylor? Are you doing all this because you think Tango wants a baby? That if you can't give him one, he won't want you?" Taylor's eyes filled with tears, and she bit her lower lip, looking away from the other woman. "Honey, you know that Tango is all in – baby or not. He wants you, Taylor, not a child. A child is the by-product of your love, not the actual love. If you have a baby, I know he'll be happy, but if you don't, I know he'll still be happy."

"I know, I know that in my heart," she said, wiping her eyes. "I do want children, but I really want to have a baby myself." Gabi nodded at her.

"Okay, honey, let's see what I can do for you. Come on, let me draw your blood, and we'll go from there."

CHAPTER FIFTEEN

Razor looked up at the reinforced concrete walls, razor wire wound tightly at the top. Six guard towers held two guards each, rifles at the ready for any possible attempts at an escape. The massive steel gates opened for his vehicle, and he rolled his window down, waiting for the guard.

"Purpose of your visit, sir."

"I'm Dr. John Diaz. I'm here as the temporary therapist while Dr. Altman is on leave." The man nodded.

"May I see your license and letter of announcement, sir?" Razor handed the man a well-worn but brand new, fake Pennsylvania license and a letter of announcement and welcome from the office of the Warden. "Thank you, sir. Please park straight ahead in the visitors' parking. You won't be allowed your cell phone inside, but if you'd like to leave it with security, you may."

Leave the phone, Razor. I've got the wires working, and they won't detect them. They're fiber optic woven into your jacket.

Razor smiled to himself, hearing the voice of Ace on the other end of the line. Whispering softly to himself, he spoke into the microphone.

"Eagle? Hawk? You out there?"

Got you covered, brother. We wouldn't leave you in there.

Razor let out a sigh of relief, not recognizing he was even holding it in. He stepped from his car, gathering his briefcase loaded with psychiatric journals and white papers. Entering the second gate, the guard walked him down a long, gated corridor, prisoners staring at him on both sides.

One on one, Diego could take any man in this yard. He was a Navy SEAL, trained in every form of self-defense and weaponry known to man. But he was smart enough to know, loose in the yard, the gangs would take him in a heartbeat, not giving him the opportunity to fight his way out.

"If you'll lay the bag on the belt, sir." Razor nodded, letting it slide through the x-ray machine. Next, he walked through and then raised his arms for a quick search.

"Follow me, sir. I'll take you to the warden's office." Razor nodded, following the man down the tiled hallway. He stopped, knocking on the door and then entering. "I have Dr. Diaz for you, sir."

"Yes, yes, of course, come in. Thank you, Ralph." The man nodded, realizing he was effectively just dismissed. "Dr. Diaz, please have a seat." Razor took the seat offered, waiting for the man to speak.

"Thank you for allowing me to fill in for Dr. Altman." He nodded, then spoke in a low, hushed tone, leaning toward him.

"The room isn't bugged, but I don't ever discount someone being able to listen some other way. I think you know the deal. Black is a dysfunctional lunatic. He cannot be released, and I just can't be sure that damn parole board is going to keep him behind bars. Hell, even Castro doesn't want him released."

"Castro, sir?"

"Hector Castro runs most of the Hispanic gangs inside the prison. Honestly, he's a pretty decent guy other than the fact he killed six gang members himself."

"Nice."

"Hey, you learn in my line of work to understand that there's bad and there's evil. Castro is bad but not evil. Black is evil and bad. Castro is actually going to be your first patient today. He's going to give you some background information and then lay the groundwork with Black that you're an easy mark, and he should trust you. He's usually an open book, thinks everyone wants to hear about his sick ideas, but with Castro in your corner, he'll be guaranteed to tell all."

"Okay, you're sure I can trust Castro?"

"I'm sure. Don't be surprised if he asks for some sort of favor, but it doesn't mean you have to give it to him. Listen, I know your history. Dr. Altman spoke to Dr. Harris, and she told her about your background. I admire the hell out of you as a SEAL, but inside this place, it doesn't mean shit."

"I understand."

"You're a big man, tall, muscular. The inmates will take note of that. This is a realm where the alpha wins. Castro is a small guy but an alpha. He surrounds himself with big betas. All I'm saying is watch yourself. If you need anything at all, let me know. None of the guards know about this, not even my secretary. We have to bury this guy."

"I'll do my best. I'm curious, though. Why not just have an inmate kill him? Maybe accidentally shoot him? Make it look like a hanging?"

"You've been watching too much television," he said, grinning. "I wish it would be that easy, but it's not. Cameras everywhere all the time. If I ask a prisoner to do this, they'll hold favors over me. It gets political and complicated." Razor nodded.

They stood and headed out of his office, the warden leading him to the clinic. Stepping inside the small office, he noticed that a guard was seated right outside. "Dr. Diaz, this is Henry. Henry, Dr. Diaz is filling in for a bit. Make sure you take care of him."

"Yes, sir," said Henry, standing to shake Razor's hand. Razor grinned at the big man, his wide shoulders barely fitting in the uniform shirt.

"I do believe you're a man that can take care of just about anything, Henry," he said, grinning.

"Yes, sir," his big toothy grin letting Razor know there was a kindness to the man. They looked up to see a man walking toward them with another guard, and Henry nudged Razor. "That's your first one, doc. Hector Castro."

"Send him in," he said, sitting in the chair in front of his desk. Being behind the desk would make him vulnerable, unable to get to the door if needed. This way, he could be assured an escape route if he had to have one, although he hoped like hell he didn't.

"Doc," said Henry, "this is Hector Castro. Hector, Dr. Diaz."

"Hey, Doc," he said, smiling at the man. Castro was a small man, probably five-foot-eight, maybe one hundred and forty pounds. His thick black hair was long, held in a ponytail, his eyes dark brown. He carried a long, thin scar along his jaw, but nothing else visible.

"Take a seat, Mr. Castro, and we'll get started."

"Mr.? Wow, that's kinda nice. Just Hector, doc."

"Okay, then just John. Tell me how I can help you, Hector?" Henry closed the door, and hearing the click, Castro leaned forward on his elbows.

"Warden told you I'm here to help?" he asked. Razor nodded. "Black's been here as long as me. When he came, he was cocky and full of himself, told everyone who would listen about what a badass he was. I put that shit to rest right away. Made him my go-to bitch."

"How nice for both of you," said Razor.

"Look, you try going twenty years without a woman and tell me other shit don't look good after a while. Don't judge me, homey. I'm helping here."

"Sorry, go on."

"Black started bragging right away about the shit he did to his sister, his sister, Jefe. It was disgusting, disturbing. That shit's fucked up. We got all kinds in here, but dudes who hurt kids aren't tolerated by any of the brotherhood. I might put a bullet in another man, but fuck around with my sister or any other kid? No fucking way."

"I can't agree more."

"Anyway, he comes to me about six months ago and says he's coming up for parole. I couldn't believe it. All he kept sayin' was he was gonna get the girl and finish what he started. The dude was sick with the shit he talked about, and I live in a place with the sickest people on the planet."

Razor felt his stomach turn, the anger welling up inside him. He wanted to just stroll down the hallway and put a bullet in Black himself, but he'd try it this way first.

"So, he comes to me askin' for a favor – access to my lawyers. Both are my cousins, kinda handy. Then they tell me about all the stupid shit he's talkin' about. Fucker is usin' my attorneys and then callin' me a greasy Mexican. Not gonna let you live long with that shit, brother. I could off him here, but I'd be the first one they'd look at. I don't want him walkin' the streets." Razor eyed the man; he wasn't telling him something.

"Why? I mean, it's admirable and all, but you're in here. He's out there, so what. You don't know his stepsister. What's it to you if he harms her?"

"Nothing to me except he knows I have a sister and threatened her if the lawyers don't come through for him. I had to make this happen in a different way. A way where he wouldn't know it was me."

"I see," said Razor, nodding. "So, it's not your generous heart. It's that you don't want him fucking with your sister."

"Is that so bad? Protectin' your family?"

"No, it's something I understand all too well," he said quietly.

"You married?" Razor shook his head. "Got brothers or sisters?" He shook his head again, although he had plenty of non-blood brothers. "Well, I can tell you I'd do anything for my sister, and I do mean anything."

"I can respect that."

"Good, then you'll understand when I say this. I'll do anything you need me to do to get Black dead or permanently here, if... if when you leave here, you protect my sister."

"Wait, what?" said Razor.

"Simple, homes, protect my sister."

"Surely you have other people out there..." He held up both hands, stopping him.

"Listen, I have gang brothers, but I can't trust one of them not to touch her. She's... she's different."

"What do you mean 'different'?"

"She's smart, man, like brilliant. Right now, she's finishing her PhD at Georgia Tech. She's gonna be a space engineer." Castro grinned from ear to ear, pride filling his face.

"Congratulations, I mean, that's great and all, but why in the hell do you need me to protect her?"

"She's blind."

"Wh-what?" Castro nodded.

"Yea, man, she's so fucking amazing. Lost her sight as a kid but didn't let it stop her. Our folks weren't around, so I took care of her. Made sure she got what she needed. Took her to school every day, got her into this special school for blind kids. She did the rest, man. Scored so high on all her tests, she got a scholarship. So proud of her, man, but he knows… knows all about her. Can't let him get to her."

"Okay, so I finish this and do what? Approach your sister and force her to come with me? If we do this, Black won't be able to touch her."

"He won't, but he got another inmate in his pocket. Dude got out last month and swore if he needed anything, he'd do it."

"What's the guy's name?" Castro raised an eyebrow at him.

"Gavin Baker."

"Where is he?"

"If I knew that, he'd be dead. Can't find him anywhere." Razor nodded again and reached out his big hand toward the other man. Castro looked down and back up.

"Deal."

"You're serious? You won't fuck me over on this? She's all I got, man. The only thing good left of me."

"I'll make sure she's safe."

"Then let's get our boy." Razor nodded but suddenly had the feeling he'd just made a deal with the devil himself.

CHAPTER SIXTEEN

"Henry! Nice to see you!" said Evan Black.

"Black."

"Oh, come on, Henry. Why don't you like me? I've been nice to you."

"Don't matter if you're nice to me, boy. You just mind your business, and we won't have any problems." Henry despised this man. His sick twisted thoughts were known to everyone in the prison.

"You better be nice to me, Henry. I'm gonna get outta here soon, and you've got a pretty little wife out there..." Henry's big hand closed around Black's throat, slamming him against the wall. Lots of prisoners made lewd or threatening comments about your family. For the most part, he ignored them, but Black was different.

"Henry? Is this my next patient?" asked Razor calmly.

"Yes, sir. Sorry about that," he said, released Black, his face beet red, gasping for air.

"No worries, Henry. Mr. Black should be careful who he says things to. Mr. Black? Come in." Evan nodded at the tall man standing before him.

"Who're you?"

"I'm the new doctor. Dr. Altman took some leave. I'm Dr. Diaz." Evan looked him up and down, and for a minute, Razor was worried the guy was checking him out.

"Hmmm, bitch probably needed to cool off. She wanted to fuck me, just like all the bitches do." Alright, thought Razor, let's start there with the delusional thoughts of grandeur with women.

"Do you find most women want you, Evan?"

"Hell yea!" he said, laughing. "Don't you?"

"Me?"

"Yea, don't you think most bitches want you, want a taste of that dick?" he asked.

"I suppose so. Women approach me a lot, ask for sex." He nearly choked on the bile rising in his throat. He'd have to play this little game to get him to open up.

"And you give it to 'em, right?" he asked with anticipation. "You give 'em what they want, and bitches are still mad at you about some shit, right?"

"I guess you're right. Never happy with what they have." Razor took a deep breath. "I mean, they all say they want it, and then when I give it to them the way they need it, they get angry."

"That's exactly what I'm sayin'!" he said with enthusiasm, almost excited at the prospect of finding someone who thought like he did.

"Is that why you're in here? Did a woman not give you what you needed?" He hated asking the question. He almost didn't want to hear the answer. It was not going to be something he wanted to know.

"Yea, man, fucking stepsister pranced around the house in these little shorts and her cheerleading uniform, mmhmm," he said, gripping his groin. "Bitch had a tight little ass. I gave her what she wanted, and she cried about it. Showed the bitch I didn't play that way. You beg me for somethin' like that, I'm gonna give it to you, and you're gonna like it." Razor tried to look appalled, tried to look as though he was shocked.

"You mean you gave her what she asked for, and she didn't appreciate it?"

"Man, you know these bitches. She asked for it in that secretive sort of way. Lookin' at me and blinking her big blue eyes, stretching a little longer than she needed before she cheered at the game. I took her first, man. Popped that cherry good." Razor took in a deep breath. He was so close to losing it. He seriously wanted to just snap the fucker's neck.

Breathe, Razor. Keep your eye on the goal.

God love Ace. His soothing calm voice brought him back to reality. Razor nodded his head.

"So, what happened?" asked Razor.

"Man, neighbor saw me take off with her in the back of the car. Called our folks, and her mom sent out the cops to look for us. Didn't matter. I got three days in that little cabin with her. Fucked every hole she had, and I got news for ya, gonna do it again when I get out."

"How are you going to do that?" he asked casually.

"Got a man on the outside looking for her for me. Bitch moved away, someplace out of state, but when I find her, she's mine, and I will finish this."

"Sounds to me like you finished everything," said Razor.

"Oh, no, man, I got so much more I'm gonna do to that little body. She won't survive, but I damn sure will, and I'll find me another little young bitch to break in."

"You like 'em young?" he asked.

"Fuck yea! Took one at twelve, little girl down the street. She was sweet too. When I'm done with little sis, gonna find one, maybe sixteen. That's a sweet age, man." Razor just nodded, biting the inside of his cheek to prevent himself from speaking.

"Listen, doc. I'm comin' up on parole, and that bitch of a sister is gonna try and say she didn't want my big dick. I need your help here. Let 'em know I'm a good guy and all. Just gave the little cunt what she asked for, then they'll see that I'm a good guy."

Razor nodded at him, pretending to write in the chart when he was actually scribbling, trying to calm himself so he didn't blow his cover on the first day.

"I'll definitely be at the hearing, Evan," he said, trying to smile.

"Fucking awesome, little bitch will see my face before she dies," he said excitedly. Henry opened the door.

"Times up, back to your cell." Evan was so distracted he didn't even razz Henry about his wife. Finally, he'd found someone on his side, a man that understood what women were like. Henry looked at Razor, his body hunched over the desk, his fists planted on the top.

"Piece a work, ain't he, doc?" said Henry.

"Yea, Henry, he's... he's something alright." Henry eyed the younger man, looking him up and down, and then stepped inside the office, closing the door. "Did you need something, Henry?"

"Don't know what you're doin' here, doc. Don't care, really. Seems to me you're doing something with Black. Now, if you're helping him, you and me are gonna meet in a dark alley. But if you're here to make sure he doesn't see light, we're gonna be best friends, and from the looks of you, if we met in the alley, you just might give me a run for my money."

Razor smiled at the man, nodding.

"You think so, Henry?" he asked.

"See, everyone thinks I'm just some old country boy without an education. Let me run it down for you, doc. I've seen a lot in my life. I'm fifty years old. I've served my country for twelve years, and my guess is you did too. Don't acknowledge. I already know. I have a degree in political science, became a sheriff's deputy, and then took this job. Keeps me closer to home for my wife. Now, I think you served, and that has something to do with why you're here. Like I said, if you're helping him, we got problems. If not, you and me are good."

"We're good, Henry, trust me."

"I will till you give me reason not to." He walked out of the office and waited for the next inmate to come down the hall. Razor slouched in the chair. This is gonna be a long fucking week.

CHAPTER SEVENTEEN

"Keep your hands up, Taylor," said Zulu, circling the tiny woman. "That's it. Keep them up in front of your face. Good, good, move quickly, honey. Speed is your friend. That's it." He stopped and turned her in front him, her back to his chest. At six-foot-six, he towered over her tiny body.

"Okay, honey, look in that mirror there. What do you see?" he asked.

"Umm, I see a man twice my size behind me."

"I'm more than twice your size, Taylor. Not every man will be, but most will be bigger than you. You are never going to win a fight or take a man my size down for good without a gun." Her face crumbled in disappointment.

"Wh-what am I supposed to do?" she asked.

"Stop me long enough to run. Do you run?" he asked. She nodded, smiling.

"I'm actually a good runner. I ran most long distances in high school and college and then did a few half-marathons in the last six years."

"That's perfect. What I'm going to do is teach you how to stop a man my size, but then you run like hell, honey. Understand?"

"Understood." Tango watched as Zulu sparred with Taylor, teaching her some basic boxing moves, and then moved on to some rudimentary tactical moves she could use to at least stop her opponent. Her small, compact body didn't have a lot of muscle mass or any kind of mass, and that could play both for and against her. If she could learn to disable someone long enough to run and hide, it might save her life.

Now, his next worry was her procedure she was having with Gabi tomorrow morning. He'd wanted to tell her not to worry about it, but he knew she was going to worry no matter what. Finally, he decided this was her body, and if she wanted to try this, he would support her.

"Hey, brother," said Whiskey, walking up next to him with Gunner and Ace.

"Hey, man."

"How's she doing?" asked Gunner.

"Okay, Zulu's just trying to teach her to disable her opponent. She's so damned tiny there's no way she'd bring down a man his size or mine. He's doing a bang-up job. I don't know if I could remain objective if it were me trying to teach her."

"I know what you mean. When Ghost taught Gracie how to use the handgun, he about lost his shit. Initially, he was against the twins teaching her, but eventually gave in to that shit and let them do their thing. I think sometimes we're just too close to it, and of course, when they belong to us, we go all alpha on their cute little asses." Gunner shrugged with a whatdya gonna do attitude.

"So why are you guys here?" asked Tango.

"Razor had his first encounter with Black." Tango sucked in a breath and waited. "Nearly killed him right there. This dude is fucked up more than even we thought. We listened to the recording. Not something we recommend for you to do."

Tango nodded, looking toward Taylor and Zulu again. She was smiling and laughing as he tried to avoid her foot kicking out at him.

"What else?"

"Razor made a friend, two actually. A guard by the name of Henry Delisle. Interesting history, but he might be an asset to Razor if he needs it. The other dude was Hector Castro, the guy in charge of the Mexican gangs in the prison. Wants Black taken down but can't do it himself because the dude threatened his sister. I'm guessing it's not like the movies where you can just shank a guy in the prison yard and be done with him. Either that or the politics are worse than we thought. Castro made a deal with Razor that he'd help with anything if he watched over his sister for him."

"What the fuck?" asked Tango.

"Yea, she's blind and a PhD candidate at Georgia Tech. Brother gave his word, and as we all know, Razor's word is good as gold. There's more."

"Of course, there is," growled Tango.

"Black made friends with an inmate, Gavin Baker. He was doing twenty for sexual assault and attempted rape. Got released early. Castro thinks Baker is helping Black look for Taylor. He was pissed when he found out she wasn't in state any longer. Castro said Black made a deal with Baker on something or has something he's holding over Baker's head, but Baker agreed to help him find Taylor and, if necessary, Castro's sister."

"So, we need to find Baker," said Tango.

"Already working on it, brother. Ace did some background work on him. His brother is a member of the Desperate Sons, the motorcycle club in Savannah. We're riding down there tomorrow, be back in a couple of days. Ghost made the call to the president; we have a good relationship with them. President said Baker's brother is a member, good standing, all that shit. Wasn't sure about any contact with him."

"I can go," he said, looking at the three men.

"Nope," said Whiskey. "You need to stay with your girl, brother. This will be fast, and we shouldn't have any issues. We'll be back in seventy-two hours."

"I appreciate it, brothers."

"Family, dude, it's what we do. Honestly, right now, I'm more worried about Razor than anyone. Dude really sounded defeated after his first day." Tango shook his head, looking back at Taylor again.

"I can't imagine the shit he's hearing. Maybe we let him take some time when he gets back. He might need it."

"Already got it primed for Bree to talk to him and give him a week to get his head back on straight, although he's gonna have to think about how to handle Castro's sister."

"I'll see what I can find on her. Maybe put some contract protection on her until we can figure out what Razor wants to do," said Ace.

"If things are on the up and up with the Despicable Sons, maybe we ask them, spread some work around. Might be seen as a goodwill gesture by our club?" Whiskey nodded.

"I'll ask Ghost what he thinks. For now, take care of the girl. We'll see you in a few days, brother." Tango gripped their hands in a manly handshake, hugging them close as Taylor walked over. They all turned with a wave and a smile as she moved to his side.

"Where are they off to?" she asked.

"Just going on a little road trip, honey, nothing big. How was the workout? Did you finally take down Zulu?" he said, grinning. The big man walked up behind her, gripping her shoulders.

Taylor swung her elbow back to his abdomen, pulling it before it hit, and then jammed her foot down hard on the top of his arch, again pulling it. Turning, she rammed a fist toward his nose and then a tiny knee in the direction of his groin.

"Oh fuck!" said Tango.

"Yea, nice job, little bit," said Zulu. "You were fast. You hit all the points, and you didn't panic. Just remember to run next time." He raised his big arms and growled as she laughed.

"You're not supposed to laugh, baby girl," said Tango, laughing with her.

"Sorry, but knowing him now, I just don't see him as all that scary. I know you can be, just not with me," she said, smiling at him. Zulu nodded, laughing with her as he gave her a brotherly hug.

"That's okay, Taylor. I don't ever want you to be afraid of me. Any man in this compound would protect you. Always remember that." She nodded as he turned and headed to the showers.

"How about some dinner, baby girl? The others asked if we would join them in the restaurant." She nodded, kissing his jaw.

"I just need to shower," she said, running her tongue along his jaw, toward his lips, opening his mouth with her wet, hot tongue. "Wanna join me?"

"Fuck, yea, if I don't, I'll have a stiff one all night."

"Let's go, Tyler. I need to be satisfied. After midnight, no sex for ten days," she said, pouting.

"Oh shit, forget dinner," he said, tossing her over his shoulder. "We're fucking until midnight."

CHAPTER EIGHTEEN

Gunner, Whiskey, and Ace pulled into the compound for the Despicable Sons, their kuttes removed and placed in their saddlebags as a sign of respect. The president for the DS club walked out to greet the three men. He looked to be in his mid-fifties, tall with a bit of a portly belly. His silver hair was cut short to his head, his long white beard resting on his chest. His fat fingers were layered in tattoos and big silver rings.

Gunner smiled up at the man. This was an old school biker, someone who was most likely raised in the old ways of how clubs were run but looked as though he was trying to attract younger members now as well, with a different mindset. He walked toward the men, his hand extended.

"Whitey?" asked Gunner.

"What gave it away?" said the older man, pointing to his head. "Had this damned white hair since I was twenty-seven. I'm Whitey. Nice to meet you, boys. Ghost called down and said we might be able to help with something. Always happy to help the Patriots out. I'm a fan of what ya'll are doin'."

"We thank you," said Gunner. "I'm Gunner. This is Whiskey and Ace."

"Come on inside," said the older man, eyeing them up and down. "What the hell is Ghost feeding you guys up there? I have some big boys in my club, but you three look like you eat, sleep, and drink your way through a gym."

"I'm actually part owner of our club gym," smiled Gunner. "Whiskey is just a badass, and Ace is just a naturally ripped fucker." Ace gave a slight grin and shook his head.

"Well, he said you were looking for Gavin Baker's brother. What's the piece of shit done this time?" he asked.

"Don't know that he's done anything yet other than jumped parole, but we think he might. He befriended a guy while locked up, a real asshole. This other guy, Evan Black, he raped and beat his stepsister repeatedly."

"His sister?" yelled Whitey.

"Yea, man, she's the woman of one of our own, and now we're afraid he's trying to get to her through Baker. We just wanna know where he is, so we can have a conversation." Whitey nodded and then called to the man behind him.

"Find Shred and tell him I need to see him," he said in a gravelly voice. "You boys want a drink? A girl?" Whiskey laughed.

"I'll take a beer, man, but got a wife at home carrying our first baby. I won't mess that shit up."

"Same," said Gunner. "A wife and a little girl at home." Whitey looked at Ace.

"What about you? You're awful quiet." He looked Ace up and down, and to Ace's credit, he didn't move.

"No thanks, not much of a talker and don't really like people." Whitey laughed and nodded.

"Not much of a people person myself anymore," he grinned. "Club used to be different when my father was president. We had girls wall-to-wall giving away head and pussy all day long. Now, most of the guys have an ol' lady or wife at home, don't want all the headaches and drama with that shit. My pops also used to run drugs. Stopped that shit when eight of our boys were killed on a run. I won't have that on my head."

"We know it's not easy, but we've got several legitimate businesses making us money. The restaurant and bar are super profitable, but it's the custom bikes and cars that really bring it in for us. We just recently opened the gym and now a clinic too," said Whiskey.

"Damn! Maybe I should send a few of my guys up to take a look at what your boys are doin'?"

"They'd always be welcome, Whitey," grinned Whiskey. He noticed a man walking toward them, mid-thirties, dark hair and eyes, his arms covered in tattoos. He looked like he'd lived a rough life, but who hasn't. His hair was longer but clean and tied back.

"You wanted to see me, prez?" he asked.

"Yea, Shred, this is Gunner, Whiskey, and Ace from the Steel Patriots. They wanted to ask you about your brother."

"What's the psycho done this time?" he asked, taking the seat next to his prez. Whiskey raised an eyebrow at Gunner, and Ace immediately started making a mental note of his body language.

"You knew he was released from prison?" asked Whiskey.

"Yea, I knew. The prison contacted me to let me know. My brother threatened my life several times while in prison, so they're required to notify me when he's released."

"Has he contacted you?" asked Gunner. The other man eyed him suspiciously, tilting his head. "He's working with another man inside the prison, threatening the life of a brother's woman." Shred let out a long breath and nodded.

"Well, if that's the case, I hope to hell you find him. I don't know about the other guy, but my brother was responsible for raping and nearly killing our cousin, our first cousin," he emphasized. "She was eleven at the time. He got away initially but then was caught doing the same to another little girl. My cousin ended up unable to testify. She was so traumatized by the whole thing, she's never spoken since then. The other girl was able to, but they only gave him twenty years because she was seventeen. I couldn't believe it."

"I'm sorry, man. We don't get to pick our blood family," said Gunner.

"Listen, I'm really sorry for your brother, but I promise if Gavin tries to contact me, I will definitely let you know. There is no love lost between the two of us." He stood to leave and then turned to the three men. "One more thing, if you decide to hunt him down, count me in."

Whiskey raised his eyebrows, and Whitey let out a long slow whistle.

"Well, I guess we're back to square one," said Gunner.

"Listen, I've known Shred for almost twenty years now. He's a good guy, and he definitely would like to see his brother locked up or dead, either one. If he says he'll help, he will."

"Ghost did ask us to mention one other thing we could use your help on since you're closer than us," said Whiskey. The other man nodded, waiting to hear what they had to say. "It's a delicate matter, but we promised someone we would protect his sister until this mess is done. She's an engineering student at Georgia Tech, but she's blind. Her brother thinks she might be in danger either from Baker or someone else that this guy Black knows."

"We can do that for you, happy to. I have two young guys who would fit in at the university and have family living close by. Send me the information on the girl, and we'll send them out first thing in the morning."

"Appreciate it," said Gunner. "Can we crash here tonight?"

"Have the rooms already made up for you. Happy to have you boys for the evening." Settled in their rooms, Gunner sent a text for Ace and Whiskey to meet him in his room.

"What do you think?" asked Gunner. Ace was the first to speak up.

"I think he was telling the truth about his brother. His voice didn't waver. His body language was true, and I got close enough to get a link to his cell phone. He's had no contact with anyone other than those here at the club." He smiled at the other two, and they grinned back at him.

"Love your geekiness, brother. Just don't let Whitey know, or we may become unwelcomed guests quickly. So now what do we do? We have no leads on Baker, and Razor is still trapped in that fucking prison job."

"Now we wait. Someone will fuck up sooner or later. We'll just be ready to stop them."

CHAPTER NINETEEN

Although Taylor's procedure was considered 'minor,' it didn't prevent Tango from pacing the waiting room, marking tracks in the flooring.

Bree walked a patient out from her side of the clinic and stood in front of Tango's pacing form. Grabbing him around the shoulders, her five-foot-ten body hugged him.

"It's going to be okay, Tango. Gabi is the best. You know that. This is a simple procedure, and when they're done, Taylor will feel better, have easier periods most likely, and has a greater chance of getting pregnant."

"I know, Bree. It's just, damn, I hate that she's putting herself through this thinking that I might leave her if we don't have a kid of our own. I'd adopt, you know?"

"I know, honey, but maybe she's the one that wants a kid of her own. Listen, Tango, most women feel almost inadequate if they can't carry a child of their own. Women who suffer from infertility or have multiple miscarriages often go into deep depressions. I can't reveal names, but I'm seeing three patients with those very issues."

"Wow, three in our little town alone?"

"It's a lot more common than people think it is. Experts might say it's all the chemicals in our food or that women are waiting later in life to have children. I don't know. What I do know is that there is a huge stigma attached to women who cannot have children of their own. Add onto that, certain men are unable to accept a child that isn't theirs. They see an adoptive child as someone else's sperm and struggle accepting it."

"I guess I can see that," he said, nodding his head. "I mean, I don't agree with it at all. Look at Gunner, for fuck's sake. He latched on to Calla the second he saw her, thought of her as his own from that moment on."

"I think that speaks more to the kind of man Gunner is, honey. Taylor just needs you to support her in whatever happens, Tango. Be patient with her, don't force the conversations around having children or not having children. Focus on developing a full life for the two of you as a couple, not as a family yet."

Tango nodded again as Gabi walked out.

"How is she?" he asked.

"She's fine, Tango. Really, she did very well. The procedure is relatively simple, and I think we got all of the endometriosis, and I was even able to remove some of the scarring. She'll bleed heavily for the next twenty-four to forty-eight hours, and then after that, she should be fine. No sex or motorcycles for ten days, but after that, she'll be fine to do any normal activity."

"Thank you, Angel eyes," said Tango with a sigh of relief. She pulled him in for a hug, kissing his cheek.

"My pleasure. Give Doc a few minutes to get her cleaned up, and then let's watch her for about an hour. After that, you can take her back to the house." Tango nodded, taking the seat behind him and placing his head in his hands. Loving this woman just might kill him. Tango felt his phone ring and pulled it out of his pocket.

"Tango."

"Tango? It's Grant Zimmerman. I'm down here at the shop to complete the final walk-through. Is there any way you or someone else could come down here?"

"I'm actually sitting in the clinic waiting on Taylor now. She just had a minor procedure. Is something wrong?" he asked.

"Well, look, someone trashed the placed again, only this time it's worse."

"What the fuck?!" he yelled. "I'll be down there as soon as I can, but I'll send someone now."

"Alright, man, we'll be waiting."

CHAPTER TWENTY

Zulu and Ghost walked into the coffee shop, kicking aside splintered wood and broken pieces of drywall. Spray paint covered the walls and floors with the words 'cunt' or 'whore,' the oven doors were ripped off their hinges, the bakery case glass smashed, the espresso and coffee machines beaten with a sledgehammer.

"Holy. Fucking. Hell," said Zulu, staring at the mess. "What the fuck happened?"

"Not sure," said Grant. "My crew chief got here early to meet with the inspectors and noticed the back door was ajar. When he went inside, this is what he found. Police noticed that the cameras out back for the shop and the bookstore have been tampered with. Someone was smart enough to freeze them on a continuous loop."

Zulu walked to the panels, inspecting the security systems. Whoever did this has some knowledge of security systems. Ace's systems were nearly unbreachable, or at least almost.

"This is gonna crush her, brother," said Ghost, looking at Zulu.

"Yea, well, hopefully, Tango can speak with her about it, but we have to assume that Gavin Baker is in the area." He pulled out his phone, dialing Whiskey's number. "Brother? We got a problem. You still at the DS compound?"

"Yea, man, we're just eating breakfast, and then we're headed home. What's up?"

"Get to a secure room with Whitey and Baker's brother if you can." Whiskey hung up and five minutes later called Ghost again.

"Ghost? I've got Whitey, Gunner, Ace, and Gavin Baker's brother, Shred, here."

"Whitey, nice to talk to you, brother. Sorry it's under these conditions. I've got a serious issue here, and I may need Shred."

"What the fuck is happening?" he asked Ghost. Ghost proceeded to relay what happened at the coffee shop and the condition they found the place in.

"We have to assume that Baker is in the area. I know Shred wanted to be a part of hunting him down. Well, I can guarantee you I'll be hunting his ass down. Only thing is, I don't want your life in danger here, Shred. I know your brother threatened you."

"My life is in danger crossing the road, Ghost. This won't make shit of a difference. Gavin is crazy and dangerous. From what I learned about Black, he's the same. I think you might need my help if for no other reason than to draw my brother out. He might be willing to help Black, but he's more concerned with killing me."

"Brother, I hate that fucking logic, but I won't disagree with you. Whitey? Can you spare him for a week or so? I'd owe you a solid, brother."

"Don't owe me shit, Ghost. You've done a lot for our club in the past. I'll send Shred and another of our boys, Crash. Already got two down guarding the girl at Tech."

"Thanks, man. I'll see you boys this evening." Ghost hung up and turned to see Zulu talking to Grant and the sheriff. Zulu was giving the best description they had on Gavin Baker and asking that no one approach him alone. Turning back to Ghost, Zulu gave him some information.

"Most likely came in between four and five this morning. Sheriff said patrols were probably starting shift change around that time. One thing Grant brought up is that there's a daycare down the street. Baker has never gone quite that young, but we may want to warn them." Ghost bit his bottom lip and nodded.

"Alright, let's get the debris cleaned up and then lock her down."

"My crew will take care of that, Ghost," said Grant. "I can make sure we cover the graffiti and just make it look like it's still under construction. One suggestion? I didn't want to tell the sheriff because, honestly, he'd fuck it up just like the bookstore. There's a second-floor storage space. You boys might want to check it out, see if maybe he was hiding up there."

"Get rid of the sheriff for us, Grant. We're going to head upstairs." Ghost looked at Zulu, his huge body next to his own, and grimaced. In these old buildings, everything creaked anyway, but with their combined weight of over five hundred pounds, it was really going to creak.

"Slow and easy," he whispered as they walked up the stairs. Zulu pulled his weapon, although he definitely preferred hand-to-hand. Ghost was behind him, weapons in both hands.

Slowly opening the door at the top of the stairs, Zulu noted the boxes stacked in the space. Boxes of cups, lids, coffee, and other supplies for the coffee shop. Walking slowly, he peered behind each stack to his left while Ghost walked to the right.

"He was here," said Zulu, looking down behind a stack. "Dust everywhere but here. A big ass print and a candy wrapper tucked under the box. Doubt very much if Taylor would be eating candy bars in her attic." Ghost nodded.

"Okay, let's get eyes on the store from across the street. When Ace returns, have him set cameras on the roof of the hardware store over there and maybe behind the building from one of the trees lining the alley. See if we can get motion sensors up here. This son-of-a-bitch thinks he's smarter than the rest of us, but we're going to teach him a few things."

"What about Taylor?" asked Zulu.

"Taylor doesn't leave the compound. If Tango can't be with her, one of us is. I want the women and kids on lockdown. We need to make sure that Darby understands why Calla can't go to school right now." Zulu nodded again.

"I hate this, brother," said Zulu. "We didn't fight in all those fucking hellholes for all those years only to come home and have our families threatened. I want both of these fuckers caught, and I want them both dead."

"I couldn't agree more," said Ghost. "I wonder if we shouldn't just arrange for an accident at the prison. I mean, if Evan is dead, Taylor is safe, and the Castro girl is protected if we track down Baker, this officially ends."

"I'm game," said Zulu.

"Then let's make a game plan."

CHAPTER TWENTY-ONE

Taylor woke lying on the sofa in the living room, sunlight filtering through the huge floor-to-ceiling windows facing the valley, the soft gray afghan tucked beneath her chin. A glass of water and a bottle of pills were sitting on the coffee table. She could hear shuffling around the house and knew that her guardian angel was home. Smiling, she pushed herself up to a sitting position with little difficulty.

Her abdomen was tender but nothing horrible. She was slightly bloated, but other than that, she actually felt pretty good. Rising, she stepped into the bathroom to change the pad, noting that there was a moderate amount of bleeding, but again, nothing like some of her periods could be. When she finished, she found Tango waiting for her in the living room.

"There's my beautiful girl," he said, grinning. "Why are you up? If you need something, just call for me." She laughed, taking her seat on the sofa again.

"You can't pee for me, Tango. Some things I have to do by myself, and besides, Gabi said I could get up and move around. It's actually going to help with the bloating." He nodded, but Taylor knew that look. He was hiding something, and it wasn't good. "Did she tell you something, something different?"

"No, baby girl. Everything she told you, she told me. Everything looks good, and there's every reason for us to be positive about starting a family when we're ready."

"Okay, then why the frown?"

"Honey, we got a call this morning from Grant. They were scheduled to do the final walk-through on the inspection of the remodel for the shop." She nodded.

"Yea, I remember, but he said I didn't need to be there. Did they change their mind? I mean, I can't go down today, but maybe I could meet them tomorrow or the day after."

"No, baby, that's not it. The shop was vandalized again, honey. We think it was someone who is working with Evan." Her face blanched, and she leaned her head back against the sofa, sucking in big gulps of air. Would she ever be free of this man?

"How... how bad is it?" she asked.

"Grant thinks he can get most of it repaired again..."

"How bad, Tango?"

"Bad. There was graffiti, broken glass, plaster. The coffee machines were broken, everything."

"What did the graffiti say?" she asked. Tango looked at her, debating whether to lie to her or tell her the truth.

"Baby girl, I don't think it matters what it said."

"It matters to me," she said, staring at him, her big blue eyes filled with tears.

"It said 'cunt' and 'whore.'" She nodded at him and bit her lower lip.

"That's Evan for sure. Those were his two favorite words for me. I mean, we know it's not him, but it's whoever this other person is that's helping him." She let out a long slow breath as if steeling herself for what would come next.

"The insurance company isn't going to be happy about another claim, and frankly, I'm not so keen on it either."

"What do you want us to do, baby girl?" asked Tango, pulling her into his side.

"I'm not sure, but for now, can we just lock it up? I want to think about it for a while, but maybe, maybe, I don't do anything."

"What do you mean, honey? Do you not want to re-open the store? I mean, it's your grandparents' place and all, and I know how much you loved working there." He kissed the top of her head, gently rubbing her back.

"I mean, I do... did love working there, but honestly? I'm exhausted, Tango. I open and close the shop every day. I'm responsible for all the baking, the ordering, the accounting, everything. It was my refuge for so many years, but maybe that's the problem. I'm seeing that it's not really a refuge for me anymore. I think I allowed it to become my cage. I was safe as long as I stayed in that little shop serving coffee, muffins, and sandwiches."

"It seems only natural after what you went through, baby girl. It's not a decision that has to be made today." She nodded against his chest.

"If... if I decide to sell it, I have to find some other way to make money," she said.

"Don't have to think about that right now, baby. Just get well now. Let us handle what's happening at the store. I'll have Grant lock it down, make the immediate repairs. For now, the locks and security stay on at all times, even when we're home together. Don't leave the house without me or one of the other boys."

"But, Tango, we're in a locked compound here."

"I know, baby girl, but it doesn't mean it's impenetrable. I won't survive if you're not safe, Taylor. I just won't. Promise me, baby. Promise me you'll keep everything locked down."

"I promise," she whispered. "I love you, Tyler."

"Love you too, my precious girl, more than you'll ever know."

CHAPTER TWENTY-TWO

Castro looked down at the man sucking his dick. If he closed his eyes, he could enjoy the feeling of the wet mouth and tongue without thinking about it being a man. The problem was this man was fast outliving his usefulness to him and, more than that, was now a liability. Unable to concentrate, he shoved him back and tucked himself back in his pants.

"What's the matter, Hector?" grinned Evan. "Got a lot on your mind? Maybe not liking my mouth anymore? I'd say I'm hurt, but I really don't give a shit."

"Watch your mouth, or I won't care a fuck about your threats. I'll have you gutted and fileted right here on the floor before lights out." Evan grinned at the man, standing so he could see that he was now sporting a hard cock. He reached down, stroking himself up and down.

"Maybe, I should make you suck me off," he said, grinning. "I mean, it's either that or when I get out, I can make that sweet sister of yours do it for me." Castro ground his jaw together, his fists clenching by his sides.

"Don't threaten her again, Black. You won't live to see my sister."

"I might not, but we both know Baker's tastes are delightfully similar to my own. We compared notes, and I must say, he gave me some amazing ideas on what to do with my sweet sister when I get out. Of course, he's already out there, helping me. Give him a little time, and he'll find her. You just wait..."

His words were cut short when the man in front of him gripped his throat with one hand, his fist tugging on his penis with the other. Castro shoved the heel of his hand against Black's windpipe, his grip on his appendage strong. Truthfully, he wanted to vomit at the touch of the man, but he was making a point.

"You utter a word about my sister again, and I will kill you, Black. You forget I have people out there as well. People who can protect her, care for her. If you so much as make one more sound about my sister, I will end you. It would be a shame since you're so close to getting out and all," he grinned. Castro knew that his words would strike the right chord with Black. His eyes grew wide with excitement, face filled with a breathless smile. He released the man, letting him fall to the floor.

"Touchy, touchy," gasped Black. "Alright, Castro, I'll play it your way for now." He stood, his pants still unzipped, his cock still hanging out. He gripped his semi-hard length and shook it at the other man laughing.

"Come and get me when you get hungry, Hector. You know I can satisfy any fantasy." He left the cell, walking back towards his own as two of Castro's men walked in.

"I don't know why you tolerate that sick boy," said one of his men.

"You know why," he said. "Make sure he doesn't connect with someone else now that Baker is gone. I want him on his own at all times." The men nodded and walked away, leaving Hector to his own thoughts. He moved to the small desk and searched through the stack of letters, pulling the one from his sister, her smiling face staring at him.

She was his entire world. When she lost her sight, his parents basically lost all interest in supporting their children. At just seventeen, he joined the Desperadoes and started to bring home enough money to support his little sister. He walked her to school every day, through gang-infested neighborhoods, made sure she was always protected. When the school recommended that she go to a special school for the visually impaired, he knew he had to do more to get the money for tuition.

And he did.

Taking any job he was offered, he excelled at the game of death. It didn't matter. His sister is what mattered. By the time she went off to college, he was heading the gang he once joined as a boy. She had no clue about his illegal activities, and he would keep it that way for many years until he couldn't any longer. Her brilliance was his undoing when she'd overheard him speaking to his men. She confronted him, and he confessed everything to her. Instead of anger, she was grateful for his love and support but would refuse to take his money any longer.

Instead, she applied for scholarships and worked part-time editing books in braille. But he never allowed her to go without. If she needed new clothes, he would find a way to get them to her. If she needed food, suddenly there was more in her grocery cart than there should be. He always watched over her, and she knew it and loved him for it.

When he was convicted of murder, he didn't want that shit to touch his sister, but she'd insisted on showing up in the courtroom to plead his case. To tell the jury that her brother was a good man who protected her and took care of her when her parents refused. As much as he loved her for that, she'd exposed herself to his world.

"Why? Why did you come?" he asked as she sobbed.

"I couldn't let them see you as a monster, Hector. You're all I have! What am I going to do now? How will I survive?" she asked.

"You're going to survive because you're amazing," he'd told her. "I've put money in a trust for you. Finish your education, hermana. Make me proud, but don't visit me again. Don't come here." She'd agreed but, of course, didn't keep her word visiting him more than a few times until he refused to see her again.

The guard appeared at his door, a clipboard in his hands.

"Morning, Hector," he said casually.

"Good morning."

"Time for your appointment with Dr. Diaz." Hector looked up at the man, confused at first. He didn't have an appointment with the man. Then thinking it wiser, he simply nodded, following him down the long corridors. Before reaching the locked doorway, he turned to see Black speaking with another man, a guard. Oh shit.

CHAPTER TWENTY-THREE

Eagle, Hawk, and Razor sat in the motel room listening to the information from Ghost on the other end of the line. If Baker knew where Taylor was, that meant that Black might know as well, and anything was possible.

"We need to end him, now," said Ghost.

"I made a promise to Castro, brother," said Razor. "I know you have his sister under surveillance, but I want to make sure I don't go back on my word. Let me speak with him and see what we can come up with."

"I know you want to keep that promise, brother, but this is Taylor we're talking about," said Ghost.

"I know, Ghost. Believe me, I know. But we don't need Castro as an enemy. He has some pretty nasty friends both inside this place and outside. If anything, I'd like to have him as a friend in case we need some of that nasty help one day."

"I get it. Really, I do," he said to his friend. "Do you think you can convince him to let this happen? I mean, we've gotta do it one way or another but seems to me we want his approval."

"I think he wants him gone. If I can convince him that we have his sister protected, he'll go for this."

"Okay, what about the warden? We know he wants Black gone as well, but a killing inside his prison might be hard to justify."

"Same as Castro. He wants him gone. I may even be able to get Henry in on this. Black has threatened his wife a few times, and the guy makes him nervous. I don't want him taking the blame for anything. I don't want his job jeopardized, but he may help us in some way."

"Alright, let me know what Castro says, and brother? Be careful."

"Always." Razor looked at Hawk and Eagle, their faces filled with concern which was unusual for their usual joking personalities. "You guys look like your dog died."

"Not funny, brother. This is a prison, Razor. If you kill this guy and somehow get stuck in there, a riot could break out. We won't be able to get in."

"I know. I know, believe me. I just need to figure out the best way to handle this with minimal disruption."

"Overdose?" said Hawk.

"Maybe. Not a bad idea." He looked at his watch, cursing. "Fuck, I gotta go. My first patient is at ten. A lovely gentleman who killed his mother because she wouldn't let him watch Jeopardy. He did, however, bury her in the backyard next to her favorite dog."

"Wow," said Eagle. "And here I thought my life was exciting."

Razor nodded and headed to his car, where he drove to the prison, parking in his usual spot. By the time he'd finished with his first patient, he asked Henry to call for Castro, saying he needed to speak with him. A few minutes later, Hector walked in, and Henry shut the door.

"My friend, we're making a habit of this," he said, smiling. "The men will think I've suddenly developed a soft side, wanting to get in touch with my feelings or something." Razor smiled, shaking his head.

"I don't think you have anything to worry about, Hector."

"My sister, Isabella, is she safe?" he asked, his face genuinely filled with concern.

"She's safe, just like I promised. We have two men watching her, guarding her apartment day and night." Hector released a heavy breath, running his hands over his face.

"Thank you. You have no idea how much better that makes me feel. My hermana is stubborn. She refused to ask for help. I know she's capable, but she's..."

"She's still your sister, and she's blind," said Razor, smiling. The man nodded.

"Now, what are we meeting about today?"

"Black. He needs to be taken care of sooner rather than later. Baker knows where his sister is located, and I can only assume he's fed that information back to him. I can't risk him getting out, and I can't risk him giving the order to kill her. There is no indication that he has approached your sister, but we need to end him now."

Castro nodded slowly, looking thoughtfully at the other man. There were a million ways to kill a man inside, but most of them had consequences that he couldn't afford to take.

"We know it's too dangerous to have you directly involved. If he's shot, there will be questions as to why we had loaded weapons on the clinical side of the prison. A taser won't kill him, but it will disable him."

"Drugs?" he said, looking at Razor.

"We think it might be the best way. Has he ever shown an interest in drugs in the past? Maybe just a casual user?" asked Razor.

"Everyone here is a casual user, my friend. What he likes more is food, in particular fish of any kind and sweets," he smiled. "Cookies, brownies, cakes, anything with sugar, and he's lined up for it." Razor nodded again, smiling.

"A man has his weaknesses. Me? I have a weakness for full-bodied women with brains, but sugar can just as easily kill a man. How do I get it to him?" asked Razor. The door opened, and Henry stepped inside, staring from Razor's face to Hector's.

"I can help with that." He smiled at the two men and then closed the door. "Folks don't pay attention to the two-way speaker on the outside. I get paid to listen and make sure you're safe. That's all. Black has been threatening me and blackmailing me for months. He likes my wife's cooking. I could make something special, have it out ready to eat the next time he leaves your office."

"You could be risking your job, Henry. We don't want to do that," said Razor.

"I appreciate your concern, but maybe it's time I did something else." Razor looked at Hector, who smiled at the older man nodding.

"You're alright, Henry," said Hector.

"Other than bein' a killer, you're not so bad either, Hector." Hector chuckled at the man, nodding. "So, what's the plan?"

"I need to think about this. Figure out the best way to make this happen. Give me a day or two. In the meantime, watch him like a hawk. If he so much as shits differently, I want to know about it." Hector nodded as Henry led him out of the office.

Razor? We think we have an idea.

CHAPTER TWENTY-FOUR

Whiskey, Zulu, and Ghost were hovered over the computer, listening to Razor's conversations with Hector. The dude appeared to be on the up and up with them, which made Ghost feel a little better. From behind them, they heard a soft knock. Cracking the door, Angel eyes peeked inside.

"Sorry to bother you, I just needed to let you all know that Taylor is resting comfortably." Ghost nodded but waved her in.

"I'm glad to hear that, Gabi. Thank you."

"Of course, no problem, I..." She heard the words over the computer and froze for a moment. Ghost looked at her again, then to Zulu.

"Baby, you know you can't talk about any of this, right?"

"Yea, yea, I know, secret spy stuff and all that, but I might be able to help you."

"If you think for one fucking minute I'm letting you go inside an all-male prison, Angel, you've lost your damn mind," growled Zulu.

"Don't growl. It's seriously unattractive," she said, kissing him. "Listen, there are a lot of poisons and drugs that can kill a person, but most are fairly traceable and could lead authorities straight to the source if they really wanted to follow this."

Ghost let out a long breath and ran his fingers through his hair, frustrated that this was so complicated. Given a choice, he'd just put a bullet in the guy, but he knew he didn't have that option.

"So, what do you suggest?" asked Whiskey. Zulu glared at him. "What? She obviously is smarter than all of us, so I'm willing to ask for help." Gabi smiled at the group of men.

"Shellfish."

"Shellfish? You want us to feed the guy?" asked Ghost.

"No, I want you to fix him a seafood meal and place it in a container with cookies nestled right alongside it. We make sure the seafood is bad. Test it to be sure it contains maitotoxin. I can show Razor, Hawk, and Eagle how to test for it. They fix the meal, make a cookie or brownie, and we inject it with the toxin as well. Since it's lying next to the food, they will assume it simply absorbed some of the toxin."

"He won't taste that it's bad?"

"Nope. People rarely can tell the difference until it's too late. If we do this and do it well, I can make sure there's enough maitotoxin to paralyze and kill him." Zulu looked at Ghost and then Whiskey, his eyebrows raised in a questioning look.

"Maybe she shouldn't cook for you anymore," said Ghost. Gabi placed her hands on her hips and grinned.

"Flatterer. Don't worry, baby. I still like your big sexy stick and enjoy my man in bed. No danger of me poisoning you."

"Seriously? You have to say that shit in front of us?" said Whiskey. Gabi winked at him.

"Keep in mind, big man, I know the sex of the baby your wife is carrying. I can be bribed." She turned and left the room, and Whiskey stood, wide-mouthed, wanting to yell out for her. Zulu could only shake his head at his wife's smart mouth.

"Brother, you two were made for each other. That shit is scary," said Ghost.

"Yep, but she's all mine," said Zulu. "What do ya'll think?"

"I think we're going to fix our boy a dinner he won't forget."

CHAPTER TWENTY-FIVE

Taylor and Tango walked in the backdoor of the barn, his arm securely locked around her waist, her body safely tucked beneath his shoulder. He maneuvered them straight into the kitchen, where George was busy preparing the evening special, a fall classic, chili.

"Sit here, honey. George, do you have any tea here? I'm out."

"Course I have tea! What sort of place do you think I run?" he said, frustrated. "What kind do you want, honey? I got green, jasmine, chamomile…"

"Green is perfect, George, thank you." He nodded, moving around the kitchen, filling the cup with hot water, and handing her the teabag. Tango watched everything she did, and when he attempted to open the tea bag for her, that was all it took.

"Tyler, baby, I love that you want to take care of me, but you are driving me crazy. Please, go check on the garage or something. I'll be fine here with George. You don't mind, do you, George?"

"Don't mind at all," he said, grinning at her. "You're prettier to look at than him. Go, get outta my kitchen and leave her here with me. I know what I'm doin' and know how to fend off an intruder."

"You're sure?" he asked, kissing her forehead.

"Yes, honey, I'm sure. Go." Tango left the kitchen, and George turned to see Taylor let out a long breath.

"Suffocatin' ya, honey?" She grinned at the older man and nodded. "He's just showin' his love, is all."

"I know, George, but seriously, I mean, I'm locked inside the house unless he's with me. Since the procedure, he won't let me lift anything heavier than a sandwich, and honestly, all this shit with my coffee shop has me really confused." George nodded, stirring the big pot once more. He set the spoon on the ladle, putting the lid on the pot. Taking the seat next to her, he took her tiny hands in his big, rough, wrinkled ones and leaned forward.

"Listen to me, honey. That man loves you somethin' fierce. Now, I know them boys sometimes don't know how to show it properly. Hell, they get those protective instincts running, and everything else gets shoved out the window. But it's how they were trained, how they were raised. He does it cuz he loves you."

"I know, George. Honestly, I do, and I'm so grateful every day that he came into my life when he did. You know, when I was a little girl, my parents divorced, and I never saw my dad again. He just left and never returned. His parents, my grandparents, owned that coffee shop. They were amazing grandparents, and I spent every summer there helping in that shop." George nodded, smiling at her.

"When... when my stepbrother..." she swallowed, looking away from George.

"I know, honey. No need to think on that now." Taylor nodded, giving him a weak smile.

"When all that happened, all I wanted to do was escape, and this was the only place to do that. I never wanted to go back. That year I spent here was the best year of my life. My grandparents let me sit in the corner and read for that first month. It's all I wanted to do. Then my grandmother made me get up and help with the food, and I found I could lose myself in it."

He nodded, standing to stir the chili again. He lifted a spoonful to her lips, and she tasted the heavenly broth.

"Mmmm, good, maybe a little more chili powder?" she said. He nodded again. "When my parents made me come home, I was so miserable. I just wanted to get back to that little coffee shop. I discovered this week that I was using that shop as my armor. It was my safe place. The place where I felt like no one could touch me, no one could hurt me, except that wasn't true at all."

"No place on earth like that, honey," said George, taking her tiny hands in his once again. "I know that sounds awful, but the truth is the world is a scary, violent place. Those men out there have seen the worst of that, which is what makes them so damned good at their work."

"I can't hide anymore, George. I almost missed out on Tyler and I having a future together because I was hiding. He's been coming into my shop for more than six months, three times a week asking for coffee and muffins, and he doesn't even like the damn muffins."

George chuckled to himself, nodding. That boy did have a serious hate for muffins for some reason.

"What am I going to do, George?" she said, looking at him, her blue eyes filled with tears. He stood once more, slicing a piece of banana bread for her to taste. She sniffed, biting back her tears, and bit into the piece of bread. "It's good, maybe more walnuts."

He grinned at her again.

"Seems to me you like what you were doin' just not where. That coffee shop has a lot of good memories for you, 'specially around your grandparents, but it also has bad memories that make you feel cemented to the floor."

"That feels like a true statement," she said, watching him.

"I got a proposal for you."

"You do?" she said, looking surprised.

"Yep. Gracie would help me every now and then with bakin' cuz I don't really like that, but she's just one person. It's hard on her now, especially with JT. What if you and she split the duties. You two help me with pastries, cookies, cakes, breads, anything related to the baking. We could even try and open the restaurant for breakfast on the weekends if Ghost is agreeable to it."

"Really, George?!" she asked excitedly.

"Really, beautiful," he smiled. Taylor stood and wrapped her arms around his waist, hugging her face to his chest. He smelled like her grandfather, and that brought a tear to her eyes. George just hugged her tightly, rubbing her back as she sniffed against his shirt.

"Fucking hell!" said Tango. "I leave you alone for thirty minutes with my woman and come back to find you stealing her!"

"Not stealing her, comfortin'. Best you keep in mind, though, if I wanted to steal her, I damn sure could," he said, winking at Taylor.

"George said I could help him bake here, maybe open the restaurant for breakfast!" she said excitedly. Ghost stood behind Tango smiling.

"Could you make those fancy coffees here, Taylor?" asked Ghost.

"Yes! I could bring the machines up here. We could do a full breakfast menu or just something light for brunch, but I wouldn't have to go back to the shop."

"Is that what you want, baby girl?" asked Tango, pulling her toward him.

"I-I think so. I mean, yes. Can I? Ghost, Tango? Can I?" Ghost laughed, seeing the excitement in her face.

"I got no problem with it as long as you know you're working for George."

"Yes! I would love to work with George. He's amazing!" George turned to the group and smiled.

"See, that's how you treat someone, respect."

CHAPTER TWENTY-SIX

Eagle and Hawk met Bree halfway between the prison and the complex in Virginia to obtain the maitotoxin and then turned right around to head back to the motel where Razor waited with Henry. Gabi wrote out explicit instructions on how to make sure the toxin was placed in the food, including warning Henry to have his wife wear gloves during and after preparation, throwing away any bowls or utensils used in the preparation.

The next day, as planned, Black was sent for his therapy session. Razor could barely contain himself during the session. Black was truly demented. He saw nothing wrong with explaining what he was going to do to, not only to Taylor but other women when he got out. As if he believed that Razor wouldn't dare tell anyone about his plans.

He wondered how someone got to this point and then remembered Taylor saying that he'd tortured and killed animals as a child. Something his parents should have taken care of. Although, all he knew was of the father's existence and then the stepmother.

"I'm curious, Evan. You mention your father and stepmother now and then, but what happened with your biological mother?" he asked. He looked up at Razor with an almost childlike excitement filling his eyes.

"Oh, I killed her."

"Sorry? Say that again," he said, leaning forward in the chair.

"I killed her. My dad was saying that she was always complaining about something, and then when I killed Mrs. Portman's little terrier, damn yappy thing, she said she was calling the police and sending me away. Dad said we couldn't let that happen, so I killed her. He helped me bury her."

Razor was stunned. He actually didn't know what to say to any of that. Taylor's stepfather knew the kind of danger he was putting Taylor in and yet did nothing to protect her.

"So, your dad just said she was always complaining, and then she threatened to call the cops on you and have you sent away, and you just decided to kill her."

"Yea," he said casually. "We decided together. Like I said, he helped me bury her."

"Sounds like a real father and son bonding moment," said Razor. Evan looked up at him with a big smile and nodded. Christ! This guy was truly off his rocker. How in the hell had no one discovered the depths of his mental illnesses?

"Yea, that's exactly what it was! My dad and I were super close after that. He was my best friend." Suddenly, Razor had a very disturbing thought. What if the father helped Evan? What if he made sure that he was alone with Taylor that weekend? Holy shit.

"Sounds like your pops was pretty cool," said Razor casually. "You guys ever share photos of the girls, videos, that kind of thing?"

"How did you know?" he said, smiling. "Yea, he bought me all this cool video equipment and camera equipment. Even helped me set up a camera in Taylor's room so I could watch her changing and playing with herself. Man, I miss that videotape. I bet my old man still has it. We used to watch it together. We had boxes of photos we took when we had our outings."

"Your outings?" asked Razor, swallowing back the bile rising in his throat.

"Yep, we'd go off together and pretend to go fishing or something and find girls. Man, we had some fun. He'd let me have them first while he took pictures, and then he'd take what he wanted. He didn't like pictures taken with him, but it didn't matter. He taught me so much!" Razor heard Ghost's voice in his ear and nearly flinched.

End this now. You don't need to listen to anymore. End it. Get out.

"Well," Henry opened the door and nodded.

"Times up," he said, staring at Evan.

"Damn, just when we were getting to the good stuff," he said, standing with a stiff erection. Razor wanted to slice that dick off and shove it down his throat but knew the method they already had in place would be just as painful.

"I'll see you next time, Evan."

"Yea, doc, love these sessions," he said, smiling as he walked out the door. He looked down to see the open container of food sitting on Henry's chair. "What do we have here? Little mama make you dinner again, Henry?"

"Stay away from my food, Black."

"Or what? I think I want to taste what the woman might cook for me while you're unavailable," he said, grinning. Henry pretended to make a move toward him and then stopped, his fists clenched at his sides.

"Fine, you take it, but you gotta eat it here. Can't take outside food into the blocks." Evan nodded, shoveling the food into his mouth.

"Oh, man, that's good! Love me some seafood!" he said, spilling food out of his mouth. He picked up the brownie like a child, almost drooling on the pastry. In two bites, it was gone, and he handed Henry the empty container. "Tell the little woman I'll be back for more."

"No, you won't," said Henry as he watched him walk away. He turned to see Razor standing in the doorway. "You okay, doc?"

"It's Razor, Henry. Just call me Razor when no one is around."

"How long before we can bury him?" he asked.

"Not soon enough."

Sometime after midnight, Evan Black found himself in excruciating pain lying in his bed. Then just as suddenly, his body couldn't move. Despite the pain, despite the agony he was feeling, his body wouldn't respond to the need to move, the need to scream. His gaze stayed glued on the ceiling, and then he heard the door of his cell open.

Looking up, he saw the faces of Henry Delisle and Hector Castro, with no expressions at all. It took a total of seventeen minutes for his heart to stop. Henry and Hector timed it. When they could feel no pulse, they backed out of the room and shut the door.

"Nice work, Henry," said Hector.

"You too, Hector. See ya around."

CHAPTER TWENTY-SEVEN

Taylor entered the big meeting room, taking a seat before the group of men. You could have knocked her over with a feather when they gave her the news. She was nothing short of stunned. Evan Black was dead – gone from the face of this earth. She'd dreamed it so many times. Wished it until she couldn't wish it anymore. Now it was confirmed that he was no longer a concern for her.

"So, does this mean that I can leave the compound?" she asked.

"Not yet," said Ghost. "We're still concerned about the man he was working with, Gavin Baker. He hasn't been located, and we know that he's in violation of his parole."

"I see," she said thoughtfully. "Okay, I mean, I understand."

Razor looked at the table of his brothers, still dressed in his suit and tie from his acting role at the prison. He'd arrived at the prison this morning to be bombarded by investigators asking questions about Evan Black and his time in therapy with the new doctor. He'd pretended to be stunned by his death and willingly gave all the information he could.

"Taylor? I need to ask you some other questions. Not about Evan, but about his father."

"Louis? Okay, but I haven't seen him or my mother in more than ten years. Their lack of support during the trial was more than I could handle or forgive, and when my grandparents died, they didn't even send a card. As soon as I was able to get away from them, I did."

"So, when exactly was the last time you spoke?" asked Razor.

"Probably Christmas, maybe ten or eleven years ago. I don't know. I guess I was twenty-four or so. So, yeah, that would be about ten years ago."

"What were they like? How did they sound?" Taylor looked at Razor and then Ghost, finally turning her head toward Tango.

"I don't follow. Why is this relevant?"

"Honey, just help us out here," said Tango. She nodded.

"Our conversations were always strained after the incident, but they weren't the best before that. My mother was easily manipulated. When my father walked out on us, her only concern was finding someone who could fill the role and provide for her and I. She wasn't loose. I mean, she didn't bring men home, but my mom wasn't a strong person."

"What do you remember about Louis Black when they started dating?" asked Razor. She shrugged her shoulders.

"I-I don't know. He was fine. I mean, there wasn't anything remarkable about him. He was average-looking, average intelligence, that kind of thing. He was nice to me. Always asked about my day, my activities. He wasn't overly affectionate, not at first."

"Tell us what you mean by that, honey," said Tango.

"I mean, at first, when they were just dating, he would wave or smile but didn't touch me at all. When they decided to marry, he immediately started hugging me more. I was fine with that, I guess. I mean, I was looking for a replacement for my father as well, and he seemed willing to take that role. It wasn't creepy or anything. He would just hold me tight. The only time he ever lost his temper with me was when I asked about his late wife or told him that Evan was acting strangely."

"Okay, when you asked about his wife, what did he say?" asked Razor.

"I don't understand why you're asking this. What does all this matter now?"

"It matters, baby girl," said Tango.

"I guess he and mom had been dating about six months, and I asked him if he and his wife were divorced, and he said no, that he was a widower. I was thirteen at the time, I didn't understand what was appropriate or not, so I asked him what happened to her."

"What did he say?" asked Ghost.

"He blew up at me. Said it was rude of a child to ask about such things and that it was none of my business. He said it was too painful for him to speak about. My mother looked at him with such sympathy I knew I'd overstepped. I apologized profusely, and he finally forgave me, but he warned me never to discuss it with Evan. That it was too painful."

"Your mom, during all this, how did she react?" asked Whiskey.

"I-I don't really remember. She didn't jump to my defense. I remember that. I think she just sort of sat there, watching it all like it was a film or something." She looked around the room, Razor's face so etched with concern, Whiskey, Ghost, Zulu, and Gunner all seated with their arms folded, and Tango gently rubbed her back.

"Someone, please tell me what in the hell is going on here," she whispered.

"Taylor, I won't give you all the details of what Evan told me in that prison, but I can tell you they were awful and not just about you, honey. Taylor, did you know, did you find out after the attack that he was filming you? Taking photos?"

"Wh-what? H-how... no, no, that's not possible." She turned an ashen color, her face completely gray, her hands started to shake, and Whiskey left the room, grabbing a bottle of water and a glass of whiskey. He set both in front of her and smiled.

"Drink, honey."

"D-did you see... did he have the video... the pictures?" she asked.

"No," said Razor. "He didn't have any of that with him there. However, he claimed that your stepfather knew about the videos. He claimed that he helped him obtain the photos and put the video equipment in your room."

Taylor's chest hurt from the need to breathe. She tried to suck in gulps of air and couldn't, her fingers starting to tingle.

"Get Doc," said Ghost. Ace nodded, sending a text to Doc in the clinic.

Tears were falling freely down her face as she rocked her body back and forth, trying to regain some sort of composure. Doc ran into the room, immediately kneeling next to her. He looked at the men around the room and saw the expressions, knowing what had happened.

"Deep breaths, Taylor. Breathe, honey," he said softly. "Good. Take a drink. Another. Okay, look at me, sweet girl." She looked up at him.

"Doc, how could he do this? My own stepfather?"

"I don't know, Taylor. That's what we're trying to find out." He sat on the other side of her, watching her for a few moments. "Can you continue?" She nodded.

"It… it makes sense."

"What makes sense, Taylor?" asked Razor.

"During the depositions, my… my stepfather said he had proof of me traipsing around the house in little shorts and my cheerleading uniform. He… he was helping his son."

Razor held back on telling her that he believed her stepfather most likely had photos and video of what occurred that weekend with Evan. He didn't think she would be able to handle that information, but he was damn sure he was going to find the box with all of it inside and destroy it.

"Why wasn't it submitted if he said he had proof?" asked Whiskey.

"My lawyers... the lawyers my-my grandparents paid for... oh my God!" Realization hit her that her grandparents were there to support her, but her own mother hadn't even bothered to come to her defense.

"Taylor?"

"My grandparents paid for the attorneys. My m-mother said they couldn't afford lawyers for me when they had to pay for a lawyer for Evan. They were worried about him. She didn't care. The lawyers told my stepfather that the things he spoke about wouldn't be admissible in a court of law. I was so young. I didn't understand. He said they were photos he took as a family, just like parents do. Taking pictures of their kids. That wasn't it at all, was it?"

"I don't think it was, honey," said Razor. "Taylor, where do your stepfather and mother live?"

"Th-they live in North Carolina the last I spoke to them. Just across the Virginia state line. But that was ten years ago, so I don't know." Razor nodded, watching her try to gather her emotions.

"Taylor? There is nothing that you could have done differently, nothing. I think Evan and his father were working together, and I think they've done it to other women. I also think Evan was responsible for killing his mother, and I believe his father helped him cover it up."

She couldn't say anything. Nothing would make this any better, nothing.

"Honey," said Doc. "I'd really like for you to speak with Bree. Will you do that for us? WIll you come with me to the clinic and talk to her?"

"I-I think I need to do that," she said quietly. Looking toward Tango, there was a sudden rush of tears, and she wrapped her arms around him. "D-do you hate me?"

"Baby girl, you're killin' me here. Why in the hell would you ever believe I would hate you?"

"I-I was so stupid. I didn't see what was happening. I..."

"You couldn't see it, baby girl. There is no way to see this kind of evil when all you're focused on is the good in people and being a teenager. If I'm angry at anyone, it's your mother for not protecting you the way she should have. I'm angry at Evan and your stepfather for taking your teen years from you. But you? Baby, I am so in love with you. None of this will change that." He kissed her and held her tightly as his brothers watched, their faces filled with concern and caring.

"Come on, honey," said Doc. "Let's get down to see Bree." She nodded, leaving the room safely tucked beneath Doc's big body. Tango turned toward Razor.

"I don't know how you stood being in the room with him as he spoke about this. I would have killed him myself," said Tango.

"Don't think I didn't want to, brother. I'm glad we've wiped him off the planet, but if I believe my gut, and I usually do, I think his father is the one creating issues with her shop."

"What do we do?" asked Whiskey. Tango looked at the men in the room, the look of death etched on his face.

"We hunt him down and kill him."

CHAPTER TWENTY-EIGHT

"I want to know how my son died," said Louis Black to the man seated across from him. He'd been filled with hope just a few weeks before. His son would get parole. He would make sure of it. Now, he was being told his son died from accidental food poisoning.

"I've told you, Mr. Black. Your son died from food poisoning. He ate a dish with seafood, and the seafood was bad."

"Why didn't anyone else die?" he asked.

"The food belonged to one of the guards. Evan, your son, actually took the food from the guard. I know you don't want to believe it, Mr. Black, but your son was manipulative and cruel."

"My son was a good boy! He had a heart of gold. He never hurt anyone!"

"Mr. Black, I won't argue with you about what was already successfully argued in a court of law, but your son was more than capable of bullying, torture, and murder. His record is clear, Mr. Black. I'm sorry that your son died, truly I am, but it was accidental and will be listed as such. As per his requests, we've cremated the body, and the remains are waiting for you."

"Cremated? I didn't authorize that!"

"No, sir, but your son did. He signed the paperwork to have his remains cremated should anything happen to him here inside the prison."

Louis Black stood from his seat, pacing around the room. His fists clenched and unclenched in anger, and the warden waited for him to do something foolish. Henry Delisle stood in the corner of the room just watching the man, understanding now how the son had become so disturbed.

"I'll sue. I'm going to sue this prison!" he yelled.

"Sir, you have the right to seek what you believe is justice. However, I will tell you that we used every means necessary to try and save your son. It was just too late. Now, if you'd like to retrieve your son's remains, Henry will walk you downstairs to collect both his remains, as well as all of his belongings."

Louis Black stormed from the room, Henry close on his heels, as he turned to give the warden a nod. He picked up the phone and dialed the number.

"Dr. Diaz," he said under his breath. "I'm calling first to thank you for covering so dutifully for Dr. Altman these last few weeks."

"You're welcome, sir, any time."

"Secondly, I'm calling to tell you that Louis Black just picked up the remains of his son. He's going to be leaving this facility shortly, but I do have a recent address if that is of interest to you."

"It is most definitely of interest to me. Please forward that to my phone if at all possible." Razor started to hang up and then spoke again. "And Warden, thank you, truly."

CHAPTER TWENTY-NINE

Today was Taylor's final visit to Gabi post-surgery and her third visit to Bree. After the team told her what they knew of her stepfather and Evan, Taylor struggled to leave the house, fearful that someone was taking a photo of her. When Tango went to the shop to meet with Grant, she couldn't make herself go inside, instead sitting at the bookstore with Darby.

She finished dressing and walked into Gabi's office for any final instructions.

"Everything looked great today Taylor," she said, smiling at her. "You can resume normal activity, including sex."

"Are you sure Tango didn't push you into that?" she grinned.

"I assure you, as much as I love your man, he couldn't push me to make that kind of decision for him, although I highly suspect I'll be receiving flowers or candy from him," said Gabi with a smile. Taylor couldn't help but laugh at the other woman.

"How are you doing with your therapy with Bree?" asked Gabi.

"I'm doing good… she's really good. I just can't wrap my head around why my stepfather did this to me, but even more so, why my mother allowed it to happen." Gabi nodded her agreement.

"I wish I understood the human psyche but that's definitely not my specialty. It's more in Bree's wheelhouse. I do know that bottling up your emotions can cause physical symptoms, so if you start feeling not like yourself, not getting enough sleep, changes in your eating habits, I need you to mention it to either me or Bree… deal?"

"Deal," she said, smiling. Taylor walked into the waiting room and through the opposite door into Bree's office. The beautiful redhead was seated at her desk, her husband perched in a chair in front of her. "Hi, am I interrupting?"

"Not at all," said Bree. "I was just trying to tell my overprotective husband that just because I'm pregnant doesn't mean I have to eat all the time."

"No, but you have to eat some time!" he barked. Taylor laughed. "Taylor, help me out, she needs to eat."

"Oh honey, I am not getting in the middle of this one. Bree will eat when she and/or the baby is hungry."

"Thank you!" said Bree, looking at Taylor. "Okay... go... I have a patient and you need to leave." She said, shooing Doc out of her office. He turned at the door, kissing her sweetly, gripping her bottom in his big hands.

"I'll be waiting for you at home," he said with a wink. "See ya later Taylor!"

"Oh my gosh! You guys are so stinking cute," said Taylor. "How long have you been together?"

"We met last October... so about a year now. We've only been married a few months though. We got married when Gabi and Zulu got married... double wedding."

"That's so wonderful. You're all such great couples... great people. I used to see you separately coming into the shop, but now it's different seeing how well you all get along." Bree nodded.

"So, how are you feeling?"

"Can't escape it can I," she said, grinning at the other woman. Bree shook her head with a serious face. "I'm okay... I guess as okay as I can be. I think I'm experiencing all the feelings, all the concerns that anyone would feel if they were in my shoes. One thing I'm really trying to come to grips with is my role in this."

"What do you mean by that... your role?" asked Bree.

"I mean, do I have any ownership in what happened? Did I walk around dressed skimpy? Was I asking for attention?" Taylor chewed on her bottom lip, unable to look directly at Bree.

"Taylor? You can't possibly think that the way you dressed justifies what happened to you."

"I-I didn't... I mean, I don't I guess, if I'm being honest, I'm just not sure anymore. I was a kid, Bree. A teenager who thought she looked cute in short shorts and miniskirts. When I made cheerleader, I was so excited, maybe I did wear my uniform too often. I don't know, I just don't know anymore."

Bree nodded at the woman and a piece of her understood the statement, but another piece of her was angry.

"Let me ask you something Taylor. Do you know about what happened with Grace?" She nodded. "Do you think Grace deserved what she got because she wouldn't let her ex-husband back in her life?"

"No! God no! I would never think that," she proclaimed.

"Okay, good. I told you about what my stepfather did to me. Do you think I deserved that because I didn't leave sooner or fight him off sooner? Maybe I wore my jeans too tight."

"No! Bree, how could you believe I would ever think that?" she said with tears in her eyes.

"Then tell me honey, how could you ever believe that you played a role in the heinous acts of your stepfather and stepbrother? It's no different Taylor, no difference at all. This is a problem for women everywhere. We are fed this bullshit that if we dress a certain way or act a certain way, the acts of men are justified." Bree took a deep breath and stood, grabbing a book off her shelf.

"This book... this book is loaded with cases of women and children who were attacked by men and the defense for the men was that the women or children asked for it by their actions." She flipped through the book, stopping at different pages. "This one... the woman was playing pool with a male friend and was shaking her hips to the music when three other men approached her, gang raped her, sodomized her, and then told the courtroom that she wanted it. This one of a fifteen-year-old girl, a gymnast who was raped by her neighbor. His defense was that she wore her skimpy leotards in her backyard while practicing her routines, practically begging him to take her."

Taylor's tears were streaming down her face, her mouth quivering from disgust and fear.

"There is more honey, hundreds more I'm ashamed to say. These women did nothing wrong. If a man showed up in that bar with skintight jeans with the outline of his penis showing, a t-shirt too tight, his muscles and tattoos showing, and a group of women attacked him, forced themselves on him. Who would be at fault?"

"The women," she said quietly.

"Do you think the courts would see it that way?" asked Bree.

"I-I don't know... I mean it's a man."

"Exactly. The courts would say that he should have been able to fight the women off or control his own erection. They expect that a woman should be able to do the same thing. Women are raped every day Taylor and some even admit to having an orgasm during their attacks. Our bodies betray us at the most inopportune moments. When your stepbrother attacked you, even if you didn't like it, even if you wanted to escape, certain physiological responses will still happen with our bodies. It can't be helped.

"Years ago, when I was first starting out, I had a young college student as a patient. He was a good size, nice muscle development, handsome... everything you would think of. He was attacked by four other men and raped. They were found innocent because they took photos of his erection during the attack, claiming it was consensual and they agreed to share photos. Now you and I both know men have less control over their bodies than women. That poor young man was stroked and prodded to erection under duress... his body reacted... he obtained an orgasm, unwillingly... and the court's found his attackers innocent. Innocent!" She said a little too loudly. Taylor jumped a little and nodded.

"You... you are not responsible for one single damn thing in all of this. Nothing! You were a child that should have been protected by her parents... instead you were exposed. You... have done nothing wrong."

Taylor wiped the tears from her eyes, nodding. Folding her hands in her lap she looked up at Bree.

"Thank you. I do understand now, I mean, I think I did before, I just needed a good reminder of it, I suppose. I think part of the guilt came from my mom and stepfather being so quick to defend Evan and then glaring at me with every clothing choice I made." She shook her head, standing to pace the room. "They made me feel guilty... made me feel as though I did something wrong. What could I have possibly done to make them feel like it was okay to spy on me, to... to film me!?"

"Nothing."

Taylor looked up at the woman.

"Absolutely nothing, Taylor. Accept that and know that you did absolutely nothing wrong. Now... now you focus on making sure it will never happen again. You're doing that by learning self-defense, by following the advice of Tango and the others. Take control honey. Control is power for you."

"Yea, control," she said, smiling and heading to the door. "I do believe I'm going to take control of something I know I can have immediately, the bedroom."

She heard Bree's laughter as she left the building, marching toward the garage. It was nearly time for Tango to leave anyway, she would just make it happen sooner. Entering through the big bay, the doors open to allow for the cool fall breezes, she waved at Razor and walked up to Tango.

"Hey baby," he said, smiling. She gripped his t-shirt, pulling him down and snaked one leg behind his, while driving her tongue between his lips, grinding against his leg. Tango let his big hands wrap around her tiny waist, pulling her closer as Razor gave a whistle in the background.

"Holy fuck honey," whispered Tango. "Does that mean you can have sex now?"

"That means I want you home, showered and on the bed in thirty minutes Tyler, thirty minutes. I'm running this show tonight." She turned to leave, yelling behind her. "Thirty minutes Tyler, don't be late."

CHAPTER THIRTY

It took Tango exactly six minutes to close shop and race home. Another eight minutes had him completely showered and on the bed as Taylor requested, the sheet folded over his middle, or at least tented over his middle.

"I'm waiting on you, baby," he called from the bedroom. His dick was ready to pound nails. Ten days without sex, even though Taylor had blessed him with more than a few blow jobs, was more than he could manage. He wanted to feel his woman's body wrapped around his own. He wanted to taste her.

He heard her shuffling in the other room and then one lean, shapely leg curved around the door frame. Tango felt his mouth go dry, and he swallowed, trying to get enough spit to actually formulate words. She was wearing five-inch blue velvet heels as she stood in the doorway, one arm leaning against the frame. His eyes traveled from those shoes up.

Her beautiful body was fully on display for him. The rich sapphire lace thong barely covering her blonde curls, the matching lace bra with no padding, just see-through material covering her breasts. Her hair was a sexy mess of curls falling to her shoulders, her lips a bright red, those thick black lashes fanning her baby blue eyes.

Tango started to move, and she shook her head.

"This is my show," she said seductively, "my performance. Tonight, you do as I say. Clear?" He nodded, still unable to form coherent sentences. Pulling out the top drawer, he heard her shuffling some things.

"I did some online shopping recently," she said casually. "It's usually not something I enjoy doing, but it seemed the best way for me to get what I needed and wanted." Taylor turned with a black silk blindfold and a pair of handcuffs. Tango's eyes went wide, and he smiled. As she moved toward him, he smiled at her pert nipples, already hard and ready for him. She slowly crawled between his legs toward his big body. Straddling his sheet-clad legs, she rubbed against his rock-hard cock and moaned, squeezing her own tits. Tango tried to reach for them, but she shook her head. Gripping one of his wrists, she put the cuffs on him.

"Above your head. Grip the headboard. Keep your hands up," she said, pushing his arms against the headboard, rubbing her tits in his face as she crawled back down.

"B-baby," he groaned.

"Shhh, I'm in control." Placing the silk blindfold on him, Tango was suddenly acutely aware of everything around him. The smell of her perfume, her shampoo, the feel of the silk against his skin. He was ready to explode. He felt the sheet being pulled from his body and moaned with need as the fabric brushed against his sensitive, leaking head.

Taylor pushed his legs a little further apart and crawled between them, kissing his inner thighs, licking her way to the big swollen balls, the cock standing at attention. Her tiny hands dug into the flesh of his thighs, tasting the man.

"Fuck, baby," he said, breathing rapidly. He felt her tongue flick out, licking each of the aching testicles between his legs, then one long slick lick of his cock, her mouth hovering over the head.

Taylor blew a long hot breath on his tip. Noticing his shiver, she smiled. Taking the big purple head between her lips, she reached up and pinched his nipples, twisting, teasing. Tango let out a slow groan, goose bumps peppering his flesh.

Her mouth came down, the hot moisture of her cavity covering his thick cock, sucking, swirling that beautiful tongue around him as one hand massaged his balls, the other twisting those nipples. His hips started to buck against her mouth, and she smiled.

"Fuck yea, that's it," Taylor pulled back, releasing his cock with a big pop. "No, no, no, where'd you go..."

"Did you like that, Tyler?" she purred against his lips.

"Fucking loved it, baby girl. Please don't leave me hangin' here," he moaned. He felt her scoot up closer on his hips and then knew she was hovering over his hard length.

"Tell me, Tyler," she whispered, her hot breath mixed with her perfume sending him into overdrive. "Tell me, honey. Do you like dirty talk?" He nodded, and Taylor grinned. She'd never felt more powerful in her entire life.

"So, you like when I tell you I want to suck your cock?" He nodded. "What about when I tell you I want to lick those beautiful, big balls of yours? Is that hot?" He nodded again. "And if I say I want to fuck you so hard, you beg for my sweet, wet pussy, is that good, baby?"

"T-Taylor, I'm begging you, honey. I'm hurtin'," he moaned. Taylor's lips landed on his own, sucking on his bottom lip, nibbling, biting, pulling roughly.

"I'm gonna fuck you now, Tango. I'm gonna fuck you like no woman has before," she said breathlessly. "When we're done, I want to feel all that hot cum," she slowly slid down his length, feeling him fill her up, "dripping out of me, then I'm going to lick… you… clean."

"Ughhhh," his moan of satisfaction as she seated herself on him was exactly what she needed to hear. Tearing the bra off, she tossed it the floor, her thong pushed to the side. Taylor rolled her hips, rocking simultaneously against his big cock, her clit rubbing perfectly against him. Gripping his head, she pulled him toward her.

"Suck my tits, Tango, suck them!" she called out. His mouth took her breasts, pulling on each delicate nipple between his teeth. When she pulled away, he felt her move.

"No, no, no," he pleaded. She grinned, turning her body, and re-inserting him in a reverse cowboy. "Oh, fuck, baby!"

"Play with my ass, honey, bring those hands down and play with my ass," she moaned, releasing his hands from the cuffs.

Fucking hell! He wasn't sure what she ate, who she spoke to, what she read, but he truly and rightly did not give a fuck. This was the hottest shit ever, and she was giving him everything he wanted. He ran a thumb around her rim, and when she moaned, he gently slid it inside her tight hole.

"Oh, yes, Tyler, that feels so full. Oh fuck, baby, I'm gonna cum, Tyler..." She screamed her release, and Tyler pumped harder, his own immediately behind hers. When he finished shaking, she lifted herself and removed his blindfold, then doing as promised, licked his cock clean, getting him ready for round two.

"How about you leave me uncuffed, baby girl, and let me run the next one," he said, kissing her. She thought about making him stay cuffed, but honestly, she liked when Tyler took control. It was part of the attraction of his big, alpha male body.

Taylor crawled on his lap again, undoing the handcuffs and tossing them to the floor. He shook his hands, settling them at her waist, but she immediately moved them to her breasts.

"I love when you touch me, when you squeeze me like you own me." She leaned forward, whispering in his ear again. "Fuck me, Tyler, fill me with your love, baby. Make me scream.

"Fuck yea!" he growled.

It was nearly midnight before they'd showered and crawled back into bed to sleep. Taylor curled into his big warm body, her head of curls tucked beneath his chin.

"I don't know what brought today on, baby girl, but any fucking time you want to repeat, have at it," he said, kissing her.

"Yea?" she said, grinning. Reaching into the nightstand, she pulled out a small purple device shaped like a tongue. "Wanna watch?"

CHAPTER THIRTY-ONE

At the breakfast table, the men all looked at one another as if they had a secret, their shit-eating grins telling each one they'd had a good night.

"Anybody wanna talk?" asked Ghost, grinning.

"Nope, not sure what came over Bree, if it was pregnancy hormones, but fucking hell!" growled Doc.

"Damn! Same," said Zulu. "I wonder if they've been talking?"

"You guys are really dumb shits, aren't you?" said Hawk. They all turned to look at him and frowned.

"What the fuck do you know?" said Gunner. "You're single. You bang a different chick every night. You fuck groups of them with your twin, and you think you're gonna tell us what came over our wives? If you tell me you've been giving her lessons, you die here, twin-boy."

"Jesus! Give me some fucking credit. I might be a man-whore, but I don't fuck around with married women, especially the women of my brothers. No dumbass. The women have been reading these steamy, hot as fuck romance novels. That shit is unbelievable."

"You read that crap?" asked Tango.

"That crap," he said, "as you so delicately put it, has been helping your women understand their own bodies as well as yours." They all eyed him suspiciously and looked at Eagle, who just shrugged.

"Talk," said Ghost.

"Look, I like to read anything and everything. I get bored as fuck sometimes working the bar or if we're on a detail like we were with Razor. If I can read shit that helps me understand women better, then I'm all fucking for it. Eagle and I aren't lucky because we're hot, although we damn sure are. We get laid because we know what to say, how to say it, and more importantly, what to do."

"You're claiming that the two of you are better at fucking than the rest of us. Is that right?" asked Tango.

"I'm saying we read; we listen; we practice, and we absorb. You can't just fuck your wives the same way all the time or expect them to show you what they want. They won't. Women aren't wired that way.

"Who writes these books?" said Whiskey.

"Why? You suddenly feel the need to read," laughed Eagle.

"Maybe, asshole."

"I've got a stack in my room. Help yourselves. I get them once the girls have all read them, so you can be damned sure if they're in my room, your wives have all read each and every one of them."

Tango looked at the twins and then around the room at the other men. Turning, he saw George smirking at them all.

"George? Did you know about this?" he asked.

"Like I said, I listen. The girls have lunch in here together and talk about the books. Don't care much that I'm in the room cuz I don't say nothin'. I can tell you, I ain't as old as they think I am cuz that shit is hot!"

"Damn," said Gunner under his breath.

"Listen," said Hawk. "All women want three things, to feel loved, to feel beautiful, and to feel appreciated. It's really that simple. Now don't get me wrong, they also each need something independently. Like, I don't know, that you love their independence or their brains or the way they make your house a home, shit like that. You guys can call us man-whores or whatever the shit you want, but when we find the women that we want to spend eternity with, we'll damn sure know how to keep them and keep them happy." The twins stood, grabbed an extra biscuit, and headed out the door.

Ghost looked at the room of men, Whiskey, Zulu, Gunner, Doc, Tango, and Razor. They were all close to the same age, between thirty-nine and forty-six. They'd all had their fair share of women, and they'd all had their fair share of failed relationships. Their current relationships were for life, so anything they could use to improve them was golden.

"No advice, Razor?" asked Tango. The man shrugged, his dark good looks giving no indication as to what he thought of the twins' advice.

"I'm not in a relationship, nor do I want to be. I think you're all fucking lucky to have the women you do. When Ghost and Grace got together, I think it gave the rest of us hope that we wouldn't be fucking bachelors for the rest of our lives. Then when Doc and Bree connected, that shit seemed a miracle!"

"Hey!" said Doc.

"You know what I mean, man. You couldn't even talk to the woman, yet now you're married and gonna be a papa. Then to have Whiskey and Zulu nab a wife? Fuck, that's epic there. Now Gunner and

Tango," he shrugged again, standing, he set his coffee cup in the sink, "makes me think even an asshole like me has a shot."

Razor left the kitchen quietly, and all eyes watched as he walked away. Ghost was the first to turn to the group.

"Keep eyes on him. That shit at the prison affected him, and I don't want any brother having negative thoughts or getting in trouble over that fucked-up situation." They all nodded, standing. "Let's meet at two and figure out how to track down Louis Black and see if we can find that other fucker, Gavin."

CHAPTER THIRTY-TWO

Louis Black looked at the small coffee shop he knew belonged to his stepdaughter. He hated the place. He'd destroyed it twice now, and yet she was still rebuilding it. He hated this town. Every time they had driven her down to see her grandparents, they'd given him the evil eye. Well, fuck them! They were dead now, and soon, their granddaughter would be as well.

The *for sale* sign in the front window took him aback. She loved that stupid little place. When he trashed it, he never expected that she would sell it. And, if she were selling it, where the hell was she? Why wasn't she still keeping the shop open?

Looking up and down the street, he finally decided to call the number for the realtor.

"Valley Realty, this is Tamara. How can I help you?" said the cheery voice.

"Hi, Tamara, my name is… Frank, and I was interested in the property on main street, the old coffee shop."

"Oh yes, that's a lovely property. The same family owned it for more than forty years. It looks a little rough right now. Some vandals really did a number on it, but I promise Taylor really took care of that property."

"Taylor?" he said casually.

"Oh, yes, Taylor Holland, her grandparents originally owned the shop and then her. Such a lovely young woman and she made the best muffins this side of the Mississippi. She's decided to sell and move on."

"I see. Well, I'd love to chat with her about the history of the building. Maybe find out what her recommendations are for refurbishing the old place."

"Oh, well, she's living out of town now, but I could call her for you if you have a list of questions."

"Did she move?" he asked, suddenly panicked that his plan wouldn't work out the way he'd thought. If she'd moved, how would he find her?

"I'm really not at liberty to say," she said calmly. "I'm sure if you have a list of questions, you could submit those to me, and I'll get them to her."

"Well, I have to be honest, Tamara. I've been burned before on deals like this, so I'm very cautious when opening new businesses, buying new buildings. You can understand."

"I do understand, sir. It's just that we don't give our owner's information away. It's why they list the property through us."

He was fuming as he sat in his rental car. This little bitch of a receptionist thought she could keep him from his prize. She had another think coming. He was the king of manipulation. Hell! He'd manipulated his eleven-year-old son into killing his wife for him. This was going to be a piece of cake.

"Are you still there, sir?" she asked.

"I'm still here, Tamara. Listen, I would greatly appreciate it if you would call the owner and just ask her if she would meet me. It can be here at the shop or anywhere really. I just want to have a conversation with her about the property. Why don't you just try to call her, and I'll hold. I'll wait for you?"

"I don't know. This is highly irregular." He could hear her mulling it over.

"Tamara, I understand how hard you work, and my guess is those around you don't appreciate all you do to keep that office running, but I can assure you I understand and appreciate everything you're doing." He could feel her mood shift through the phone and smiled.

"Alright, hold, please."

"Of course," he grinned. It was so close. So close he could feel it, feel her. It would only take a moment, and he would grab her and have her to himself. He'd teach her a lesson about leading men on. The same lesson he'd taught her mother almost seven years earlier.

They'd been estranged for years now, so no one even contacted pretty little Taylor when her mother died. Hell, most of their friends knew nothing about her. She'd been so compliant, so willing to do whatever he asked, whatever he needed, just so she would have a nice house and not have to work. Fuck, she'd sold her own daughter for the chance at a life with him.

Stupid woman. Stupid, stupid woman. They all were, really. They all thought they could withhold sex, shelter their pretty little pussies from men like him and his son. Reality was, they were all whores. Every last one of them. He looked out the window of his car at the people passing by on the sidewalk.

A woman with two children in a stroller, her jeans so tight he could make out the outline of her vagina. Her sweater was snug across her breasts. She wanted to be fucked and fucked rough. Even the older woman across the street, her black dress pants and casual shoes, trying to look demure. Except what she was really saying was, 'there's a tiger under here.' Yea, they all wanted it.

"Frank? I'm sorry to have kept you for so long. I spoke with Taylor, and she's willing to meet with you at a restaurant called Club Steel. It's a great place with good food. It's about ten miles from Main Street. She said she could meet you there around seven if that works for you."

"I can't thank you enough, Tamara. I just know this is going to seal the deal for me."

He hung up the phone and smiled. Yes, indeed, he was going to seal this deal.

CHAPTER THIRTY-THREE

The men were all seated around the conference table, laughing and joking as Ghost finally called order.

"We have several things to discuss, so let's get to it," he said.

"Ice? I guess Amanda went back to school?"

"Yea," he said, looking like he'd lost his puppy. "She only has one semester left, but she said she'd be back at break, and then when she's done, she'd like to have a job again. Sing a few nights a week if we're still willing."

"Are you fucking with me? She brought more people in on karaoke night than we've had in a year! She can fucking sing any time she wants to. In fact, maybe we use her as a headliner? Let her do one night a week and maybe look into other bands during the busy seasons?"

"I like that idea," said Tango.

"Me too," said Zulu as the others nodded as well.

"Great, we'll talk to Amanda when she's home from break. You two an item now?" asked Ghost.

"No, yes, I don't know," said Ice, shaking his head.

"Wrap that shit up," said Hawk, eyeing the man. "She's beautiful, sexy, and a voice like a fucking angel. How long do you think she's gonna last out there?" Ice growled but knew the other man was right. He'd need to make his intentions clear with Amanda when she returned.

"Is the showroom complete?" he asked Tango and Razor.

"Just about," said Razor. "We've got six bikes ready to be placed in the front, and probably another four will be ready by Christmas. The one we're working on for Sturgis for next year's rally is going to be fucking epic! We've been asked to do a bike to bring awareness to veteran suicide, so we're doing a theme bike called 'the 22.'"

"This thing is going to be fucking amazing," said Tango. "It's going to resemble the 1984 Harley Davidson Torque. Four thousand RPM, v-twin. We're even doing the cylinders in aluminum instead of iron like the original, quad pipes. It's gonna be epic, and the design on the tank? Best Razor's ever done."

"Thanks, man," said Razor, grinning with a half-hearted smile. Gunner looked at his friend and then at the other men as Razor looked down at his lap.

"You okay, brother?" asked Ghost.

"Yea, yea, fine."

"Fine isn't okay, brother," said Gunner. "You've been different since you got back from the prison. If that shit's eatin' at you, let's get it out there." Razor looked around the room at the faces filled with concern. Turning, he noticed that Tango was the one who seemed most worried.

"Listen, that shit was evil, pure fucking evil. I know, I know that a few of you listened to the recordings. I hope like fuck you never do, Tango, or Taylor. I don't understand how someone gets to that level. How you go from being a normal human to being whatever that was." Doc frowned at his friend and then spoke.

"He didn't just turn, Razor. That's a man who was born slightly wrong. His wires were crossed at birth. I think you tack onto that his father was all about the father-son bonding moments, and this guy couldn't help turning out the way he did. I'm not saying we have sympathy for him because I sure as hell don't. I'm saying that you can't understand that evil because, for you and me, it's incomprehensible."

"What about Castro's sister?" asked Tango.

"The DS guys are still watching her. They said she sticks to herself, no surprise. She's got a nice little apartment off-campus. Goes to class, records her sessions, and then types any homework or papers in braille or using audio services for her computer. Said she's definitely a loner. They saw one guy who looked like he was following her home from class, but when they questioned him, he was just hoping to get a date."

"She lives alone?" asked Zulu.

"Yep, her and a hundred- and thirty-five-pound German shepherd," grinned Razor. "The guys said they had to make nice with the dog, so he didn't bite their asses."

"I don't want to be a jerk here, but how the fuck is she gonna be a space engineer if she can't see?" said Hawk.

"Castro says she plans on reviewing the formulas and plans from home. She's already spoken to NASA as well as some private contractors, and they're willing to hire her. I don't know. It's all above my head," said Razor, shrugging.

"Okay, clinic and gym both doing good?" asked Ghost.

"Gym is stellar. Zulu has more clients than he can handle for the self-defense, fighting, and boxing. We might need to hire someone to help," said Gunner.

"Yea, man, I didn't expect so many people willing to drive for lessons. That shit is crazy," said Zulu, shaking his head.

"Okay, put some feelers out to some of our ex-teammates. Maybe we can get a few new members in here," said Ghost, grinning.

"Clinic is great," said Doc. "Bree is busier than ever, and the people further up the mountain are definitely glad something is closer than the little place in the valley." Ghost heard a small knock on the door.

"Enter!" he yelled.

"Enter? Really, honey?" said Grace with her son perched on her hip.

"Sorry, baby," he smiled. "You need me to take him?"

"No, Tamara from Valley Realty is on line two for you. She said it's important, and you would understand." Ghost nodded at his wife as she closed the door. Hitting the speaker button on the phone, he spoke.

"Tamara? It's Ghost."

"He's here. Asked specifically to speak with her and wanted to meet her. Wouldn't take no for an answer, Ghost, and he's creepy even on the phone."

"Don't engage with him in person. Tell him she'll meet him here at seven. Don't tell him anything else."

"No problem," she said.

"And Tamara? No one else. Don't tell the sheriff," he said.

"You have my word, Ghost. I owe all of you for the help you gave my dad when he was being evicted. Good luck."

"Alright, boys, we have a welcome party to plan."

CHAPTER THIRTY-FOUR

Louis Black found Club Steel easily. The bright lights made it simple to see from the road. There were only a few cars in the parking lot, but that would play in his favor. He was ready to drag her little ass out of here and have some fun. Opening the big double doors, he was pleasantly surprised by the smells of good food and soft music playing in the background.

He looked toward the bar and saw a tall, well-muscled young man washing dishes. He gave him a slight head nod.

"Sit wherever you like, man. Someone will be with you in a minute." He nodded again and chose a table nearest the door, sitting in a seat where he could watch her face as she walked in. Behind him, there was a table of men, and at another table was a man and woman eating their dinner.

He could barely contain his excitement. She would be shocked to see him, probably even happy, running to give her dear old stepfather a big hug. He would deliver the sad news that her mother passed and offer to comfort her, offering to drive her home. If she protested, saying she was fine to drive, he would just make sure she wasn't.

"Can I get you anything?" asked the waiter.

"Just water," he said quickly.

"Dude, this is a fucking bar. Now, if you have issues, order a soda. I don't give a fuck. But order something other than water." He looked up at the man, prepared to give him an earful, but when his gaze traveled along thick, tattooed muscles, he swallowed.

"Soda. Doesn't matter what kind," he said quickly. Louis turned back to the door, waiting for the moment she would lay eyes on him. Looking down at his watch, he frowned, seven-o-nine. She was late. He didn't like tardiness.

"Hello, Louis," said the sweet voice from behind him. He leapt to his feet, holding out his arms.

"Taylor! Oh, honey, it's so good to see you," he said, stepping forward. Taylor took a step back. "Taylor? What's wrong? Give me a hug, honey."

"She doesn't want a hug," said the big voice behind him. Louis turned to see a large man staring down at him. If he thought the waiter had muscles, this guy had muscles upon muscles. His dark brown hair was cut close, his beard trimmed, but that anger flashing in his face told Louis he was in trouble.

"Wh-who are you?" he said quietly.

"Me? Oh, I'm the man who loves her. I'm the man who is going to marry her and give her children. And I'm the man who is going to kill you for what you and your fucking derelict son did to her."

Louis felt his pulse pounding in his head, the beat rapid and without mercy. Drops of sweat were forming on his forehead, and he desperately wanted to wipe them away.

"My son was not a derelict. He was sick. He was getting better when he died mysteriously in prison."

"He didn't die mysteriously," said Razor, standing from the table behind them. "I killed him."

"Y-you, no, you horrible person! I'll have you arrested!"

"You will do no such thing," said Razor. "I sat there and listened to your son's confessions of his sick, twisted mind. I heard about what he did to this beautiful woman, his fucking sister! I heard what he did to the neighbor girls. I heard everything. Every. Fucking. Thing, you sick, perverted piece of filth."

"Taylor, let's just talk, honey," he said frantically. The other men rose from the table, and he noticed how very large each one was.

"We have nothing to talk about, Louis. You are sicker than your own son. You convinced him to kill his mother. You helped him spy on me, abuse me, violate me. You killed my mother." His face went white, the look of shock filling his features.

"H-how…"

"Because we're fucking good at what we do," said another large man. This one was tall and well-built with longer salt-and-pepper hair, his beard gray as well.

"I'm going to leave you here with my friends, Louis. When I leave here, I will never think of you or your son again, ever. Whatever twisted cells your DNA contains will no longer taint this earth. You will die. I, however, will live a very long, very healthy, very happy life with the man I love. A man who is more man than you and your son could possibly comprehend." She stood on her toes and kissed Tango, walking back toward the steel doors where Grace and the other women waited with George.

"She's a whore!" he said, spit flying from his mouth. Tango only grinned at the man. He could say anything he wanted; it wouldn't change the outcome. "She made my son do those things. Prancing around the house in her little sleep shorts, her cheerleading uniform. Slut!"

"She knew we were watching. She knew it! Started touching herself, pointing her pussy right at the camera!" he screamed. Zulu took a step and gripped the throat of Louis Black, lifting him off the floor. Tango smiled at his friend.

"Don't kill him yet," he grinned. "I need to have some fun."

"Take him to the storage shed behind the garage," said Ghost. Zulu wrapped a big, beefy forearm around Louis's throat, dragging him, kicking and gasping for air, to the small shed. It was barely big enough for all the men, but they didn't seem to mind the close quarters.

"Found some things in the trunk of his car I think you should see," said Ice, setting two boxes on the workbench.

"Those are my things!" yelled Louis.

Ghost nodded at Tango to open the boxes, feeling as though it wasn't his to see. Inside were hundreds of photos, videotapes, and DVDs. Sitting on top were several photos of Taylor, most likely taken in the cabin considering the condition of her tiny body. Tango could barely breathe, barely control the anger bubbling up inside.

"She's a sweet little thing, isn't she?" he said, staring at Tango, licking his lips. "I knew she would be tasty. I just knew it. Evan had so much fun with her while I photographed everything, and then I had to have a taste myself."

Tango turned from the man, closing the box. He gripped the edge of the workbench and then swung a big fist at the man's head. His head snapped back, the crack of vertebrae and jawbone echoing, blood flying from his mouth.

"You can't kill me!"

"I can," he growled, "and I will." Picking up the huge wrench, he slammed it against the side of Black's head, then, taking the hammer, made a few well-placed swings yet not quite killing him.

"I've spent a career of protecting those that needed it, killing those who harmed others, and I have never regretted one of my kills, never. You will not be the exception, you piece of shit." Tango leaned forward, his big hands braced on his knees. "Tell your demon spawn piece of shit hello when you see him in hell." He fired three shots into his head just to be sure. The others simply stared, watching.

Tango stood and let out a long slow breath. It was done. His woman could sleep knowing that neither her stepbrother nor stepfather would get to her. Ghost gripped his shoulder and squeezed.

"Go home to your woman. We'll take care of this." Tango shook his head.

"My kill, my burial. What you can do for me, though, is burn those boxes. I don't want to see even a sliver of a photo."

"I'll take care of it," said Ace, standing in the doorway. "Give them to me." Tango nodded, handing the man the two boxes, and watched him walking toward the woods. Twenty minutes later, they saw the huge blaze from one of the firepits and sighed with relief.

"It's done."

CHAPTER THIRTY-FIVE

Taylor held her breath as she walked away from Louis Black and through the steel doors with Grace; Bree, Kat, Darby, and Gabi waited on the other side, George standing in the hallway. Each woman kissed her cheek, but it was George's big grandfatherly arms she needed around her, and he gladly wrapped her up, hugging her to his chest.

Her shoulders shook with sobs filled with fear and hatred, memories and regrets. Years of pent-up anger, hatred, and shame spilled against George's shirt.

"It's alright, little bit," he said, rubbing her back. "It's all gonna be alright now. You let it out. You just cry until you can't cry no more."

"Oh, honey," said Grace, rubbing her back. "Don't make yourself sick, Taylor."

"I-I wanted to vomit when I saw him," she whispered. Stepping back from George, he took her shoulders and moved them into the kitchen. "I looked right into his face and felt the fear, the pain all come back."

"You remembered?" asked Bree. Taylor nodded.

"I remembered," she whispered. "I remembered everything. I remembered him being in that cabin and touching... touching me."

"Oh God, honey," said Bree, reaching for her hand.

"No, no, it's okay. Don't you see, all this time, I blocked it all. It was like a movie in my head. I wake up with all this damage to my body, but I don't have a clue how it got there. The images in my head were even worse than reality. I needed to remember some of that but remembering that his face looked down at me, took pictures of me. I can live with whatever is happening out there right now."

"Should we just wait here, George?" asked Darby.

"Nope," he said, leading the way from the kitchen. "I've got the grill going at Gunner's place. Axe is watching it for me while he keeps an eye on the kids. Let's head over there, and we'll finish dinner. I would suspect the boys are gonna be hungry when they come back."

Taylor nodded as they followed George across the lawn to Darby and Gunner's home. Opening the door, they laughed, seeing Axe's tall, muscled body standing with Wade and Tyler on each hip, JT clinging to his leg, and Calla running in circles singing a song. He looked up at them with a terrified expression.

"How do you guys do this?" he said. "JT won't let go of my leg for me to walk, and if I move, he's gonna fall!"

"Honey," said Grace. "He's a baby with a lot of butt padding right now and a very short distance to fall. Nudging him a bit to get him to sit isn't going to kill him."

"But I don't want to hurt the little guy. And these two, geez! Angel eyes, I adore you, but seriously, don't ever have another fucking kid with Zulu. These kids are like fifty pounds!"

"Awww," she said, grabbing Wade. "They're just big, growing boys."

"Did Calla give you any trouble?" asked Darby sheepishly.

"I don't know. Do I still have lipstick on my face?" he asked, horrified. Darby laughed, nodding. She grabbed a baby wipe and wiped the lipstick off, smiling.

"Don't worry, Axe. It's all good practice for you when you find a woman," said Taylor. "Axe? What's your real name?"

"Not much of a difference," he grinned, setting Tyler down. "Axel, Axel Mains."

"Tell us your story," said Grace, grinning. "I mean, I know you came over to our club after all that trouble with the Warriors, but what's your story?"

"I smell a set-up," he said, staring at the women.

"Best you answer, boy," said George.

"Okay, I was in the Army for eight years. I wasn't Special Forces, but I did three tours. Loved my time, but it was also time for me to do something else. When I joined the Warriors, I thought I would have a brotherhood again. Turns out it was more like a prison. Best decision I ever made was helping Ghost with Scar. Couldn't be happier that I am here," he grinned. "I don't know my parents. I lived with my older sister and her husband. I was an oops baby. She was nineteen years older than me. She was great, a little hovering, but great," he grinned.

"How old are you?" asked Taylor.

"Uh, why?" he asked suspiciously.

"Just curious. Don't panic."

"I'm twenty-nine, almost thirty." He looked at the grins on the faces of the women and stood, carefully maneuvering around the kids. "I think I'll go help George with the grill."

"He's cute," said Bree, laughing.

"He is," said Darby. "I was just thinking. I mean, we have several guys single here. Razor, Ice, Axe, Ace…"

"Our sweet Ace," said Grace, smiling.

"I know," said Taylor. "He's so darned cute, but wow, is that guy hard to get to know."

"Yea, plus we have Blade, Skull, and oh yea, the hormone twins." The ladies all let out a laugh.

"Maybe we should make this our ladies club project," said Grace, smiling. "I mean, we're all learning so much from those books, or at least I am."

"Me too," said Taylor. "The other night was a success!" The women all clapped, laughing.

"I don't know," said Bree. "I'm not so sure we should interfere in their love lives. I wouldn't want any of them to think we're pushing them into something. I like the idea of letting nature take its course."

"I'm not saying interfere," said Grace. "More like… help it along if needed." Gabi looked at the other women and then out on the patio.

"I'm in, but I say our first project is George," she smiled. That brought loud cheers and smiles to all the women. Taylor stood and looked out the window.

"Something is burning in the woods," she said quietly.

"I'm sure it's something the guys are doing," said Grace. "Let's get the side dishes done for George. I'm sure the boys will want to eat when they return." Taylor nodded and turned toward the women.

"Thank you. Thank you all for being here. You're the most amazing group of women I've ever met, and I'm proud to call you my friends."

"Girl power!" yelled Gabi. And the chorus rose.

"Girl Power!"

CHAPTER THIRTY-SIX

"Do you think we need to worry about Gavin Baker?" asked Ghost, staring at Razor.

"Yes, I don't know, man. I know I can't let Castro's sister be out there on her own while he's still free. He's violated his parole, so there's a BOLO and warrant out for him, but they're not gonna waste a lot of manpower. I know Castro is just some gang member who killed other gang members, but at his core, he did everything for all the right reasons, and there's a piece of me that respects him."

"Understandable," said Tango. "We all know what it's like to protect those we love. Seems to me he was just a kid himself, suddenly in charge of his kid sister. I'm not saying I agree with what he did, but I understand why he did it."

"Alright, let's just watch out and just make sure we're checking in with DS boys. Are Shred and Crash on their way home?"

"Yea, man," said Razor. "Crash said he might head toward Tech just to make sure he didn't spot his brother. Figures if he's there, he might try to come for him and leave the girl alone."

"Dude is solid, man," said Tango. "I mean, he's willing to let that lunatic come after him instead of a girl he doesn't even know." Razor nodded once again.

Darby walked into the kitchen with Calla right on her heels, the long brown curls held back today in a purple and gold bow, her little blue jeans and sweater with her chucks making her look older than she was.

"Uncle Tango!" she yelled, leaping into his arms.

"Hey, pretty girl," he said, kissing her cheek with a wet raspberry. "What are you doing today?"

"Mommy said since it's Saturday, I can go to the store with her for a while."

"Why you goin' to the store, babe?" asked Gunner.

"I told you," she said with her hands on her hips. Gunner wanted to say he remembered. He just truly did not. "The guy who writes those books about motorcycles and motorcycle trips? Really? Geez, Gunner, you guys were the ones who asked me to carry them. He's coming into the store. Turns out he lives only a few hours away. We want to talk about doing a book signing for his new book coming out this month, *Adventures in Color – Touring in the Fall on Your Bike*. It's beautiful! All these amazing pictures of places he toured last fall. He started up in Canada and worked his way down. It's stunning!"

"Damn, Darby!" said Ghost. "You got him to do a book signing?"

"That's what we're talking about," she said, nodding. "I'm hoping he'll be the first of many. It could be a really big deal for the bookstore. Come on, Calla. Gotta go!" She kissed Gunner as he slapped her behind. Darby jumped with a little yelp.

"Go wait in the restaurant, baby," she said, turning back toward Gunner. She walked back toward him as he leaned against the cupboard, his long legs crossed at his ankles. For a minute, he was worried she might be pissed. Instead, she reached her delicate hand toward him, rubbing it up and down his semi-hard length. Standing on her tiptoes, she let her tongue follow the line of his mouth.

"Keep that in mind for tonight, big boy," she grinned, turning and winking at the other men. Gunner swallowed, straightening himself.

"Holy shit, that was fucking hot," said Tango.

"That's what I'm talking about," said Ghost. "That's the kind of shit happening in my house too!" Hawk and Eagle stood, shaking their heads together.

"Read the fucking books!"

CHAPTER THIRTY-SEVEN

Over the next few weeks, Taylor and George worked together to create a new brunch menu for the weekends, along with breakfast for during the week. She took on the duties of baking and making the coffees, and he kept the duties of any full breakfast menu items.

Taylor had never been happier. Fall was in full force, and the colors were vibrant, stunningly so, the weather cooler with deliciously crisp breezes. As Halloween got closer, the team closed one Sunday and took the entire group to a pumpkin farm where they rode hayrides, picked apples, and of course, bought pumpkins.

The twin boys dressed as Oompa Lumpas from the movie *Charlie and the Chocolate Factory*. JT dressed as Prince Charming with Calla as his princess. It was adorable. Bree and Gabi were both over their morning sickness and both already sporting little basketballs for bellies.

When they decided to begin the planning for Thanksgiving, the guys decided they would get in on it this year as well, vowing to do a fried turkey as well as the classics. Tango looked around the room and didn't see Taylor.

"Anybody know where Taylor is?" he asked with some concern. Shoulders shrugged, and then she walked in the front door with Doc trailing behind her.

"I'm pregnant! I'm pregnant!" she yelled. "We're having a baby!"

"Way to keep a secret," said Doc, laughing.

"I know. I know. I just couldn't!" Tango stared at her wide-eyed, his mouth hanging open as if to say something. "Tyler? Tyler, we're having a baby, honey."

"A baby? We're pregnant," his whispered.

"Well," she laughed. "Technically, I'm the only one pregnant here, but I will gladly take that if you're with me." He lifted her gently against him, kissing her lips, claiming her mouth.

"I love you, Tyler."

"Oh, my sweet baby girl, I love you too. Marry me. Marry me, Taylor."

"Yes," she giggled. "Thanksgiving Day. I'll marry you Thanksgiving Day." He nodded, hugging her tightly once more. The girls all hugged her as well, the guys giving Tango pats on the back. As the women talked about baby showers and holidays, the guys huddled together.

"Did you read the first book?" asked Gunner quietly.

"I finished it last night on my tablet," said Ghost. "Some of that shit is pornographic! I'm telling you, I was so hard at one point I thought I would embarrass myself on the sofa next to Grace."

"You didn't like it?" asked Zulu, staring at this friend.

"Loved that fucking shit!" growled Ghost. The others laughed, nodding.

"Okay, then, let's keep reading because I can tell you for damn sure there were some things in that book that I had to stop and think about positioning to get my head wrapped around it. I will be doing some of that shit," said Tango.

Ace walked toward the group, nodding at Razor.

"What's up, man?" he asked.

"Shred from DS is on the line for you. Says it's about Isabella Castro." Razor nodded, following Ace to the communications room, Tango and Ghost close behind. Placing the phone on speaker, he addressed the other man.

"Shred? It's Razor, brother. What's up?"

"My fucking brother is what's up," he said, sounding winded.

"You okay?" asked Ghost.

"Yea, I'm, damn, that fucking hurts!" They could hear a woman speaking in the background and the sounds of medical equipment.

"Are you in the fucking hospital?" asked Razor.

"Yea, bastard got the drop on me. Stabbed me in the side, but I'm gonna be fine if this damn doctor will stop poking me!" he yelled. Ghost and Razor grinned.

"What about Isabella? Is she okay?"

"She is, man, but she's shaken up. He had her pinned in her apartment. She was terrified when we finally got in there. She's not harmed, but she doesn't want to be alone. I can stay…"

"I'm on my way," said Razor, walking out of the room.

"Did he just say he was on his way?" asked Shred.

"Uh, yea, man, he's on his way. You need me to call Whitey?" asked Ghost.

"No, Crash called him. I'm fine. Really, I am, Ghost. Crash is sitting with Isabella at our hotel. Once I'm cleared, I'll take a cab and meet them. She'll be safe until Razor gets here."

"Okay, man, thanks. What do we do about your brother?"

"Oh, that's easy. I'm hunting his ass down and killing him."

CHAPTER THIRTY-EIGHT

Razor arrived at the hotel outside of Atlanta at two in the morning. He was tired, hungry, and pissed off. They'd done everything they could to protect Castro's sister. Somehow Gavin Baker still got to her. Obviously, despite the fact that Evan Black was dead, Gavin was going to follow through with his promise.

He tapped on the door that Shred and Crash had indicated, and the other man opened the door, waving him inside.

"Where is she?" he asked. Crash pushed a finger to his lips.

"She's in the adjoining room. We left the door connecting us cracked, but she needed her own space, brother." Razor nodded at the other man.

"You okay?"

"Will be," he said, letting out a loud hiss as he lay down again. "Get some sleep, man. You look exhausted."

Razor took the other bed in his room, crashing immediately. His head was spinning with what he had to do tomorrow or technically today.

He needed to convince Isabella Castro to let him take her somewhere safe. Yet, he knew she would most likely object.

As light filtered into the room, he felt something cold and wet against his cheek. Brushing it away, he turned and then felt a sudden weight against the bed and his side. He jumped to his feet, reaching for his weapon as the huge dog tilted his head, staring at him.

"Fucking hell," he said, letting out a long breath.

"Taco?" He heard the breathy, sultry voice and stilled. "Taco, where are you, boy?" Holy shit, who was that? No. No, God wouldn't do this to me, he thought. He wouldn't make this woman have that sexy voice, not Castro's sister.

She pushed open the door, calling once more.

"Taco, are you in here, boy?" She stilled immediately, her head lifting. "Crash, is that you?"

Razor was glued to the carpet. Isabella Castro was a fucking bombshell. Long dark brown hair, big brown eyes with the thickest black lashes he'd ever seen. Her hourglass body was made for loving with curves he could grip and grind against. Her tits easily double Ds made his mouth water. But her ass, that beautiful, plump juicy ass, made him ache.

"This isn't funny," she said in a weak voice.

"I-I'm sorry," he said. Her head turned quickly toward his voice.

"Wh-who are you? Taco!"

"It's okay, Isabella. It's okay. I know your brother, Hector. He asked me to make sure you were safe from this man, Gavin Baker."

"And do you have a name, friend of my brother's?" she said, smiling.

"Oh, shit, sorry. Yea, I'm Razor. I mean, my friends call me Razor, but my name is Diego Salcedo."

"Diego," she said, grinning. "I like both those names. Razor is very edgy, dangerous. Diego is sexy. Are you sexy, Razor?" He nearly fell to his knees. Yea, I'm fucking sexy, and I want to sex you up, beautiful.

"I-I guess I'm okay," he said, grinning and then realizing she couldn't see his grin. In fact, it suddenly hit him that all his physical attributes that he used to lure women in wouldn't work. He couldn't use one of his killer smiles, his trademark gazes, or his moves on the dance floor. What the fuck was he supposed to do now?

"Can I, can I touch your face, Diego?" she asked.

"Y-yes," he said, clearing his throat. He stepped closer to her, stopping within arm's length, but Isabella moved a step closer, her breasts now touching his chest. He nearly groaned aloud, his cock instantly jumping.

She lay her long, lean fingers against his face, delicately tracing the lines of his jaw, gliding one long index finger down his nose, following the curve of his lips, and back up to his eyes. Then she let both hands glide through his hair, gripping him tightly.

What the fuck was happening here, he thought. Was she going to kiss him? How in the hell would he explain this to Castro? Suddenly, she pulled his head within inches of her sweet mouth, and he waited. Then he felt it. Her knee connecting to his groin. He moaned and doubled over, gasping for air.

"What in the hell! Why did you do that?" he shouted.

"Tell my hermano I don't want his drug selling, crime-ridden vermin protecting me. I can do it myself."

EXCERPT from RAZOR

"Let me out of this truck!" she yelled, straining against the seatbelt and pushing on the door. Poor Taco whined in the backseat, his cold nose laying against her neck. Razor looked at the woman beside him and smiled, her curves straining against the long-sleeved t-shirt, her black leggings making that beautiful ass look positively edible. She was a feisty one, for sure. All that Latin temper wrapped in a body made for sin.

"Nope, and if you try to jump, you'll be dead in no time. I'm doing seventy-eight, and we're riding an edge of a cliff, so have fun flying."

"Ohhhh, you're so frustrating! I don't want my brother's criminal, drug-dealing, murdering friends helping me! Take me back to Atlanta," she yelled.

"Let's get something straight, Bella."

"Don't call me that!"

"Right, let's get something straight, Bella. I'm not one of your brother's drug dealers, gang members, or even lackies. I'm not a fucking criminal. I met your brother while I was working as a therapist in the prison."

"A... a therapist," she repeated softly.

"That's right, sweetheart. It's not my full-time job. It was just temporary for a friend. My full-time job is designing and creating custom motorcycles and cars. I work for the Steel Patriots motorcycle club. I've never broken the law and don't intend to start now. I'm a retired Navy SEAL. I'm thirty-nine years old, never been married, no kids. I don't drink to speak of. I don't gamble, and I don't do drugs. If there's anything else you want to know, ask. But do not ever fucking call me a criminal or low-life again."

"I am here to help you, to keep that beautiful ass of yours safe."

She was quiet for several minutes, and he was grateful for the reprieve, if only for a few minutes. Her head angled slightly toward him, and she spoke.

"And what else would you like to do to my beautiful ass?"

OTHER BOOKS BY MARY KENNEDY YOU MIGHT ENJOY!

REAPER Security Series
Erin's' Hero
Lauren's Warrior
Lena's' Mountain
Sara's' Chance
Mary's Angel
Kari's Gargoyle
Rachelle's Savior
Adele's Heart
Tori's' Secret
Finding Lily
Montana Rules
Savannah Rain
Gray Skies
My First Choice
Three Wishes
Second Chances
One Day at a Time
When You Least Expect It
Missing Hearts
Trail of Love

My SEAL Boys (connections to the REAPER Series)
Ian
Noa
Carter
Lars
Trevor
Fitz
Chris
O'Hara

Strange Gifts Series
Dark Visions
Dark Medicine
Dark Flame

Steel Patriots MC Series
Ghost – Book One
Doc – Book Two
Whiskey – Book Three
Zulu – Book Four
Gunner – Book Five

ABOUT THE AUTHOR

Mary Kennedy is the mother of two adult children, has an amazing son-in-law, and is grandmother to two beautiful grandsons. She works full-time at a job she loves, and writing is her creative outlet. She lives in Texas and enjoys traveling, reading, and cooking. Her passion for assisting veterans and veteran causes comes from a strong military family background. Mary loves to hear from her readers and encourages them to join her mailing list, as she'll keep you up-to-date on new releases at https://insatiableink.squarespace.com. You can also join her Facebook page at Insatiable Ink.

Dear Readers,

I love hearing from you and encourage you to visit my website Insatiable Ink. Leave me know your thoughts and ideas on new books or expanding on characters. It's also a safe space to give your own feelings, like those of the characters. I love reading about how you relate to the stories because as we all know, there's a little of each of them within us.

I look forward to hearing from you and hope you enjoy other books in my collections.

Explore... and enjoy!

www.ingramcontent.com/pod-product-compliance
Lightning Source LLC
Chambersburg PA
CBHW071459170626
811CB00007B/2630

9 781716 559525